THE FAIR VISION

A Frontier Story

THE FAIR VISION

A Frontier Story

ELEANOR STEWART

Five Star
Unity, Maine

Five Star Western
Published in conjunction with Golden West Literary Agency.

Cover photograph by Holly Lidstone.

December 1999
Standard Print Hardcover First Edition.

Five Star Standard Print Western Series.

The text of this edition is unabridged.

Set in 11 pt. Plantin by Juanita Macdonald.

Printed in the United States on permanent paper.

Library of Congress Cataloging-in-Publication Data

Stewart, Eleanor.
    The fair vision : a frontier story / by Eleanor Stewart. — 1st. ed.
    "Five Star western" — T.p. verso.
      p.   cm.
    ISBN 0-7862-1897-5 (hc : alk. paper)
    1. Mayflower (Ship) — Fiction. 2. New Plymouth Colony —
Fiction. 3. Pilgrims (New Plymouth Colony) — Fiction.
4. Indians of North America — Massachusetts — Fiction.
5. Massachusetts — History — New Plymouth, 1620–1691 —
Fiction. I. Title.
PS3569.T462 F35   1999
  813´.54 21—dc21   99-041703

For my husband,
Maurice Greiner,
and for my daughter,
Karen Kritzer

Prologue

"The Queen is dead! Long live the King!"

King James I, having been ruler of Scotland for thirty-seven of his thirty-eight years, relished the repeated chant as he proudly rode his horse through the streets of London, its buildings hung with cheerful banners. Old Queen Elizabeth had finally died in the year of our Lord 1603, and Henry VIII's grandson, her half-nephew, was now James I of England, Scotland, and Ireland.

The new King not only intended to unite the two countries of England and Scotland but also felt extremely confident that he could bring peace to the western part of Europe. Son of Henry Stewart, Lord Darnley, the second husband of his Catholic mother, Mary of Scotland, James had been raised a Presbyterian by his regents. Elizabeth had imprisoned his mother when he was a year old. He had immediately been made King James VI of Scotland. He would never see his mother again and, at twenty-one years of age, would lodge only a small protest when she was beheaded. He did not propose that anything should stand in the way of his life's goal: to become King of England.

Once safely crowned, he shook off his relationships with his loyal Scottish ministers and appreciative Scottish subjects and only once returned to Scotland during the rest of his life. The kings of France and Spain, England's traditional enemies, became his preferred company.

His first act was to end Elizabeth's feud with Spain. Later, when Sir Walter Raleigh got into a controversy with the Spaniards while searching for gold in Guyana, James was easily persuaded by the Spanish ambassador to have Raleigh beheaded.

James was no traveler and had little contact with even his English subjects. His absorbing affection for hunting, a sport which had endeared him to the Scots, was not particularly appreciated by the English. The King had become more and more withdrawn, performing perfunctorily the affairs of state. He had, of necessity, to act as head of the Church of England, while his wife, Queen Anne, repeatedly pressed Catholicism on him. Still, he'd remained basically a Presbyterian. However, when goaded by another Protestant sect called Separatists who wished freedom from the Anglican church, he had resented their interference. While the Puritans' main goal was to *reform* the Church of England by "purifying" the people in it, these Separatists wanted a new kind of worship and new churches of their own. In his late fifties, he'd reacted against them much as an old cat would take a desultory swipe at a mouse. He had jailed some and driven others of their group to Holland.

This was the situation in 1620 when James contemporaneously allowed remaining Separatists to quit England and go as pilgrims to the wilderness of the New World. He had even signed the charter for their land. Little did he realize that through this act against his enemies the blood lines between Great Britain and North America would be guaranteed forever.

Chapter One

The town crier's lantern swung back and forth as he bellowed into the fog. "Five o'clock and all's well!"

Candles in cottages and warehouses along the wharf began to flicker through the drifting mist. The sound of running feet echoed on the cobblestones, and shadowy figures started to move about on nearby ships. The Barbicon quay and the harbor beyond were crowded with sailing vessels of all sizes, rocking in rhythm like the seagulls with each wave. Here and there the muffled tinkling of a ship's bell marked the time.

Across from the wharf two drunken stevedores staggered along gurgling chanteys and jostled each other into a pub. Sparrows dropped out of the damp haze and started pecking at refuse on the street. A new day was beginning in the port city of Plymouth.

Gradually the stillness was penetrated as drays, wagons, and carriages started jockeying for position on the dock where a large, square-rigged ship, the *Mayflower*, was due to weigh anchor this gray morning, September 9th, 1620.

In the distance a group of five persons approached, two men in front, followed by a woman, a girl, and a boy who lagged behind, kicking at a stone as he walked along.

"Come, Joseph, hurry on," the girl called. The boy booted the stone into the water. "Are we really going t' cross the whole bloody ocean this time, Priscilla, and never come back? We've started out on the *Speedwell* twice before!"

"So we have, laddie . . . and watch thy tongue! This time for certain the ship'll *not* come back!" She spoke forcefully as

9

if more to convince herself than the boy. She looked down at her brother, putting her hand on the child's shoulder. "Look around thee one last time, Joseph, for 'tis never again thee'll be seeing England!" Her voice caught a little. She watched a wren dart out of a rose bush across the street and disappear into a tree. "Will there be birds in this new world, Mother, do ye think?" she asked the woman in front of her.

Her mother pulled her shawl closer around her shoulders. "We can't be sure, Priscilla, but if there be trees for savages to hide in, there will probably be birds," she teased, with a look at one of the men in front of them. "Thy father insists it will be a paradise."

"Oh, come now, dear Alice," William Mullins said, calling back. "Ye know we all agreed on this voyage." Then he muttered to his servant who was carrying a large sea bag over one shoulder and a crate of chickens with the other hand. "Birds. These women do fuss about nothing."

Carter nodded with a wink, one man to another.

Mullins watched as the women walked up alongside him. They looked bright and winsome for this gray morning and for having spent the last two weeks in a small seaside inn. Alice, his wife, was wearing her rose silk with her hair in a braided crown the way he liked it. Priscilla, their eighteen-year-old daughter, was dressed in a lovely gown of spring green. Although both women were tall, they were different otherwise. Alice had light-brown hair and blue eyes. She was broad-shouldered and elegant in the Nordic manner. Priscilla was small-boned and delicate, with hair the color of summer daisies and dark-brown eyes like his own. They were women to make a man proud.

"Come now, we must get aboard," Mullins said, pretending gruffness.

Alice tossed her head, but Priscilla gave him a smile with

that special sparkle in her eyes.

"Do not bother thyself about me, Mister Mullins," his wife remarked. "We shall reach the ship before the three o' ye, like as not." She passed him with an impudent glance.

She was saucy, that one, he reminded himself, remembering how she'd insisted on bringing along her mother's wedding gown, the lyre her grandfather had played upon, and the French écritoire handed down from his side of the family. Furthermore, she'd personally supervised the loading of their goods on the ship in Southampton when the *Mayflower* and the *Speedwell* had first embarked. She was a saucy one, that she was, but he liked her for it.

They moved on along the wharf under the prows of myriad vessels anchored in port. The smell of fish, drifting in from the water, saturated the air. As they approached the *Mayflower*'s dock, the crowd and the clamor grew. Sailors and stevedores shoved their way peevishly among the people. Barrels, sacks, hogsheads, fishermen's nets, sails, and other gear drying on the wharf made progress difficult. Hawkers selling fruits, sweets, and muffins cried out their wares. Pigs grunted in their pens, and a parrot on top of a sea chest squawked at everyone who passed.

They dodged a sailor with a heavy trunk on his back, who nearly knocked Joseph in the water.

"Mind where you're going, tar!" Mullins shouted into the uproar, but the man made no answer.

Priscilla was aware by the strange look on some faces that the onlookers thought of these voyagers as daft folk, going to a wild, empty land, inhabited only by hostile savages. She lifted her chin, proud to be one of the Separatists with the courage to leave England as it was under King James. The rumor that he might send his soldiers to fetch their religious group to jail, as he had done before, was probably responsible for the large crowd, she reflected uneasily. Although the King had given his word that they would not be molested if they left the country at once, still everyone knew him to be unpredictable.

Nor had they left the country "at once." They had departed Southampton in July and had been forced by circumstances to put back into harbor at Dartmouth and again at Plymouth. And they had been here in Plymouth for two weeks—plenty of time for the King to have heard of their presence!

Priscilla's father hurried them along toward the comparative safety of the ship.

"Hey ho!" someone called behind them, and they turned to see Paul Ashby, Alice's jolly brother, and Mary, his little bird of a wife. Mary threw her arms around Alice.

" 'Tis a long way ye've come!" Alice exclaimed with a loving look at them. She tenderly took her brother's hand.

"Ye think I'd not come to see thee off again?" he replied, scooping Joseph up in his other arm.

"Ye *will* come back!" Mary asserted, as if her saying it firmly would make it so.

"That we will, Mary, dear," Alice said softly, knowing they would probably not meet again.

"We will send for ye," Mullins added.

"Do take care, my dears." Mary embraced Priscilla. "I want to be at thy wedding," she added wistfully.

Priscilla laughed. "That will, indeed, be too long for thee to wait."

"Not for a beauty like thee." Mary shook her head.

"Ye have no idea how stubborn and choosey the girl is," Mullins remarked, speaking with a smile but with a sting of truth in his voice. "And now we *must* embark!" he said, pulling Alice's arm.

12

"I've brought ye some fruits for the journey," Mary quickly broke in, "and some sweets . . . and some rosemary from the garden." She handed the basket to Alice. "Stay well, and send us a letter back as soon as thee can."

Alice waved and looked back until the crowd finally separated them.

The thrill of departure seized Priscilla again. She took her mother's arm, saw her smile, and felt her quiver with excitement.

As they neared the gangplank, Priscilla looked up at the *Mayflower*. The ship seemed to be half bird and half fish. She was quite impressive with her shining wood hull, her high fo'csle, and lofty stern. "A beautiful square-rigger she is"—Priscilla's father described her when he had been commissioned to assist in chartering a ship for the Separatists—"ninety foot long, twenty wide, with an eleven-foot deep hold. Her masts pierce the sky . . . eighty-five and ninety feet toward heaven!" he had said.

" 'Urry on there," Coppin, the second mate, called down from the top of the gangplank where he and Clarke, the first mate, were checking the manifest.

The family had started up when a drunken sailor pushed his way past them and lurched into the two mates.

"Ahoy there, the *Mayflower* . . . ahoy!" he shouted into the crowd.

"Churl! No business 'ave yer 'ere!" Coppin blocked his way.

The tar reeled and hiccuped. "Now, matey, don't yer be tellin' this Thomas Shipley 'ere yer didn't sign 'im aboard. I've got me papers right 'ere." He fumbled about and gave a twisted, surprised grin, finding them on top of his pack.

"Well, yer late," Coppin said, studying them. He looked up sharply. "Get yer blasted scuppers into the fo'csle!"

Shipley didn't move. He fell back unsteadily, staring at the passengers. *"Women!"* he finally shouted. "What kind of a farrago is this?" He spat, narrowly missing Coppin's shoes. "An' *kids!* I ain't sailin' with . . . *no . . . women!* Bad luck." He made a floundering turn and attempted to go back, but lost his balance as the first mate snatched his papers.

Coppin jerked Shipley's arm. "None o' yer balkin', flunky. Now move aboard or Clarke 'ere'll 'ustle yer 'indquarters with a belayin' pin!"

Shipley staggered slowly along, turning to make a face at the two mates.

Mullins then stepped up to Clarke and presented his papers.

"Good day, Master Mullins," the first mate said, reading, and then announced to Coppin, checking off the manifest: "William Mullins, good wife Alice, daughter Priscilla, eighteen years, six-year-old Joseph, and servant, Robert Carter. Sorry, sir, but with all the passengers, your cargo of shoes had to be stowed in the ship's hold. Captain's orders."

"Well, I trust ye stowed them with *care,*" Mullins stated. "It's a right valuable freight!"

"There's near a hundred o' ye to be quartered in the main cabin now that the *Speedwell*'s not goin' with ye."

Mullins groaned as he moved his family aboard, trying to shove through passengers and sailors. Sea bags, animal pens, trunks, kegs, and cooking gear hindered their passage. Overhead, furniture, hampers, and large crates were still being hoisted aboard by cable and lowered into the hold.

Mullins caught at a crewman passing by and held out the two valises he was awkwardly carrying. "Here, take these," he said. "It's worth six shillings to ye."

The tall young fellow looked puzzled. "Could be," he replied, staring at Priscilla, admiring her openly. Her penetrating eyes, golden hair, and regal grace seemed to have transfixed him.

She looked back at him calmly, a little amused. *He has the appearance of a gentle bear,* she thought, *with his broad shoulders and russet-colored hair.*

He started to talk, stammered, and then continued, his eyes on her father. "I might be persuaded to do it for naught."

Mullins turned back to Clarke. "Your man here is impudent. Speak to him!"

"That's John Alden. He's aboard as ship's cooper and carpenter. He's the one put beer, butter, water and beans, salt pork and beef, and maybe even yer shoes in the barrels and casks he made and tends on the voyage. He's the one made the longboat for yer explorin' an' fishin' an' such when ye reach the New World. Has charge of the rations, too."

Priscilla saw Alden look down, embarrassed at the attention.

"An' if the ship breaks up in a storm or 'its a iceberg . . . a' I'm not sayin' 'twill or 'twont," Coppin pitched in with a wink at another sailor as he passed. " 'E'll do a mite o' carpentry on 'er and she'll be fit again. 'Andy man, there! 'E's aboard by the demands o' the law." Coppin nodded proudly. "No bag-toter, 'im. Knocked Squint on 'is 'ead in the tavern there last night." Coppin winked at Priscilla. "I won ten shillin's on 'im."

Priscilla turned away. A common brawler, she thought, but he didn't look it. There was a certain pride and humor in his shyness, and if he had charge of the rations—and was the ship's carpenter . . . ? Priscilla glanced again at him out of the corner of her eye. He was looking straight at her, as if knowing her thoughts!

She saw her father start to brush aside the sailor talk as the first mate interrupted him. "Most important man on the ship, barring the captain and the mates." He clapped Alden on the shoulder.

Priscilla couldn't help a smile as Alden flushed and looked away.

"Well, now, is that so?" Her father dodged a stevedore with a large coil of rope on his shoulders. "My apologies. I thought ye to be one of the sailors. We'll have much need of your services building our homes if ye're to stay with us on the other side."

Alden shook his head negatively. "I have no plans to remain."

As he spoke, a dark-haired, attractive young girl worked her way toward them. She stood by Alden's side, waiting for him to notice her. He turned.

"Would ye be so good as to help me find my trunk?" she asked. "Everyone else is busy."

Alden looked at her, taking in the round face with the cloud-soft eyes, the lovely figure under the blue lace gown.

"Certainly," he said, "and thy name? Is it on the trunk?"

"That's so. Desire Minter. Governor Carver's grand-niece." She tossed her head with a quick glance at Priscilla.

Alden hesitated a moment, looking from Desire to Priscilla and back. "Probably thy trunk is below." Then he turned to Mullins. "I'll be glad to tote thy bags . . . and ye, miss,"—to Desire—"just follow me. We're *all* going below."

Chapter Two

The confusion in the main cabin of the *Mayflower* was appalling. The area was about twenty-five by eighty feet and had been used to store cargo on previous voyages. There were two small cabins that Alden said were being held for the Separatists' Governor Carver and his family and for Elder Brewster and his.

Priscilla stood on the steps overlooking the chaos. "Almost a hundred folk" had to be crowded into the remaining space, Clarke had said. It was difficult in the dim light to differentiate people in this seething mass from large crates, trunks, barrels, sacks of food, heaps of linens. How could it be possible for so many to exist here for even a week— let alone the three or four the ship would take to cross the ocean?

They made their way through the commotion, stumbling and catching themselves with the rocking of the ship. The Mullins family did not have far to go to find their designated space, one near the companionway. It had fresh air and easy access to the deck as one advantage, even though there was only a space about eight feet by eight feet for the four of them. Carter was assigned to the aft area, at the stern of the ship, with the other servants. William went with him to see that he had a suitable location.

After Alden went on to show Desire Minter her space just outside the governor's cabin, Alice and Priscilla proceeded to arrange their luggage.

"Barely room for the four of us to sleep," Alice remarked. "Why don't ye take Priscilla and Joseph and go above," she said to William, when he returned. "There's not room enough for all of us t' be working. I'll be right along."

Mullins gave a relieved smile, and the three of them started up the companionway. Once up on deck they began looking for friends. Across the crowd they saw Elizabeth and Stephen Hopkins and Captain Standish with his short, erect stature, his carrot-red hair, and his shy little wife, Rose.

Suddenly Joseph, who had run to the side, shouted: "There! Down on the dock . . . there's Wrassle Brewster!"

Priscilla and her father hurried to see. There were five people approaching the gangplank. The man in front was wearing a billowing purple cloak and a hat crested with a yellow feather. Tall and thin, he walked with an authoritative stride but glanced furtively behind, as he guided the woman beside him firmly by the elbow and hurried three little boys along.

"It doesn't look like William . . . but yes, it is," Mullins said, moving toward the group as they came up the gangplank. The man handed his papers to Clarke. The mate studied him curiously, then brightened and nodded.

"Elder William Brewster! I didn't recognize ye!"

Brewster seized the mate's arm. "Not so loud, my good man. We may be followed." He looked back apprehensively.

"Aye, aye, sir, but ye do look different than when we last saw ye . . . when ye came in on the *Speedwell.*"

Clarke took the manifest from Coppin, checking it off. "Elder William Brewster, good wife Mary, two sons, Love, nine, and Wrassle, six,"—he shook his head as he spoke the boys' names—"and the orphan boy, Richard More, six years old. Move on over there, sir, we're getting ready to sail."

Mullins hurried across to meet his friend, followed by Priscilla and Joseph.

"William!" Mullins called. "We missed thee, the last two

18

weeks. Did ye find safe haven? Ye slipped ashore almost before we docked here."

"Yes, indeed. An old friend from Cambridge days sheltered us."

Mary Brewster joined them, giving Priscilla a hug.

Just then a man came hurrying across the deck. He was broad-shouldered, handsome, graceful, and poised, about thirty years old.

"Thanks be to heaven, ye're safe!" he exclaimed to Brewster.

"*Bradford!* My dear son." Brewster embraced him. "It's a joy to see thee! Good that we are here together." He smiled at Mullins. "We three, all name of William!" He turned to Priscilla and Joseph. "And good to see thee, too," he said, giving their hands a squeeze.

They were joined by a gray-haired man of sixty or so, whom Brewster also greeted warmly. "Governor, in faith I'm happy to be back aboard with thee," Brewster said. "I and my family."

Governor Carver grasped Brewster's arm tightly. "I feared King James's men would take thee prisoner again and ye would miss the sailing."

Others of the Separatists gathered around with fervent welcomes, Captain Miles Standish and his wife, the Hopkins family, the Tilleys, the Whites, and Dr. Fuller and his wife.

The governor was studying Brewster. "We almost did not know thee in that wig and that disguise." He laughed. "Little chance of anyone recognizing thee in *that* masquerade!"

Brewster took his wig off, embarrassed. "I had to wear it. We were warned. Luckily we found good friends here. After having to put back into port twice, I'm sure we'll all be grateful to heaven when we are safely and definitely at sea."

Bradford put his arm around Brewster. "We must get

thee and thy family below."

Bradford and Mullins started to lead the way through the crowded deck.

Brewster pulled back. "Where are thy wife and son?"

Bradford nodded slowly toward the bow of the ship where Priscilla saw her friend, Dorothy Bradford, standing at the rail. She was looking shoreward.

"We . . . we decided to leave the boy with Dorothy's mother," her husband said. "He wasn't well when we came into port, ye know . . . and his being only five, and with such a long voyage. . . ." His voice drifted off. "Dorothy is already saddened by the separation. I keep assuring her he will join us next year when our houses are built and we have shelter, and she agreed it is best, but now she seems to regret the decision."

"I am so sorry to hear this, William," Priscilla heard Elder Brewster say softly, as, with his family, he made his way toward the companionway.

Suddenly a shrill scream shot above the noisy throng. Priscilla and her father turned to look toward the commotion, and Joseph started to run toward the rail. "Come back, son," Mullins ordered, catching his hand.

They could see a fat, frowzy woman dragging a boy up the gangplank by the ear. The child was kicking and yelling, but the woman held on.

"Fie on ye! What's to do with ye, boy! Come along now!" Her shriek was at the same level as the boy's scream. The man in front of her had another boy by the hand. Paying no attention to the disturbance behind him, the father handed his papers to Clarke, who announced: "John Billington and good wife Ellen! John, six, and Francis, eight."

Francis, breaking free of his mother, stuck his tongue out at Coppin. The mate pretended not to notice. The boy glanced up to see if his parents were watching. Then he waggled his thumbs in his ears and gave Coppin a kick in the shin.

Priscilla observed this, curious to see the mate's reaction. It was like seeing a pantomime.

Coppin, too, checked to find out if the parents were watching, quickly caught the boy behind the knee with his foot, and sent him sprawling. "W'at 'o, laddie," he said, laughing loudly as he picked the boy up, "not got yer sea legs yet? Now more's the pity. Look sharp, young 'un, so's ye don't fall a second time. There might be none there to catch ye!"

"Clever rascal, that Coppin," Mullins remarked. "Could be, Joseph, ye'll learn a few things on this voyage . . . some good . . . maybe some bad . . . but ye'll learn about living, for sure. I'm thinking we all will," he said, turning to look at Priscilla.

Just then Mrs. Billington simpered up to Coppin as he dusted off the boy's coat. "Prithee, thanks fer takin' care o' the boy."

With that, Priscilla saw her father wink privately in her direction, and she bit her lip to suppress a smile. Joseph looked at them, puzzled.

As the woman was talking, young John Billington dashed among the passengers, poking his head out between this one and that, finally climbing up on one of the twelve cannons.

"Francis!" he shouted to his brother. "Come catch me!"

Francis went running after him, crashing into bulwarks and barrels, and tumbled headlong into two sailors hauling on a sheet.

Above them, Priscilla caught sight of Captain Christopher Jones coming out of a cabin and standing at the rail of the poop deck, looking at the scene below. He was a big, burly man of middle age, broad shoulders filling out his uniform smartly.

"*Hawse out and blast!*" he roared. "*Mis*ter Clarke! Get those *pukestockings* below. *Mis*ter Coppin, take over those boys! Jyp there and Squint, lash down the ordnance! And ye there, Coppin, throw those brats in irons, if they don't behave. Get the rest of the passengers aboard. We haven't got till All Hallows Eve, blast it all!"

At that moment, John Alden and Desire Minter emerged from below decks and approached Clarke. Priscilla watched attentively, although her father had started to leave.

"Mistress Minter has a request to make of ye," Alden said.

"Ye see, Mister Clarke," the girl gave the mate an alluring smile, "when we were on the *Speedwell*, the unwed maidens had a cabin of their own, but *here. . .*!" She waved a delicate hand toward the companionway. "I really don't think young ladies should be expected to . . . live . . . down there with all those *men!* It's not seemly! An influential man such as thee can find us more suitable quarters . . . I just know!"

By this time everyone on deck was watching and listening with interest.

The first mate's stiff posture wilted a little. "Ye'd have to get Captain Jones's permission, and I don't know where he'd put ye, even if he be of a mind to help. Alden, why don't *ye* relay the lady's message to the captain?"

Priscilla saw Alden glance in her direction.

"Which one is Captain Jones?" Desire interrupted.

Clarke motioned. "That's him. Up there. . . ."

"Thank you, sir." Desire gave him a short curtsey and left, crossing the deck. Making her way through the passengers, she started up the narrow steps of the ship's ladder to the stern castle, her skirts and petticoats waving in the wind. Priscilla heard her father gasp as he grasped her arm in disapproval.

"Captain, sir . . . ," Desire called.

Clarke, horrified, had followed her. "Mistress Minter! Come down from there! Passengers aren't allowed. . . ."

The captain turned and saw the girl near him. "What the . . . *Clarke!* What the devil is going on?"

"I'd like to speak with ye, sir," Desire said, climbing another step closer. "Since ye are in charge of this ship, I thought ye could help us."

Clarke tried to pull the girl down, but Jones waved him away.

"Well, miss, what is it? We're near ready to sail."

"Ye see, sir, there's little privacy down there below decks, and that cabin is just full of *men!* And I declare . . . I don't know how we're going to live together without some . . . ah . . . untoward happenings." She gave him a warm, intimate smile. "Ye do understand, I know."

The captain squirmed, seeing the many eyes on him from below. "Yes, indeed . . . yes . . . I can see how that might upset ye young maidens. Humph! Tell the lasses to come topside. They may use *my* cabin."

"Oh, I didn't mean *that!*" The girl seemed truly surprised.

"It won't be the first time I've bunked with the mates. Now get below. We're about to cast off."

The first mate offered her his hand, helped her down the ladder, and gave her a slight bow as she turned to leave. As she passed John Alden, Priscilla saw her give him an impudent look. Priscilla heard her say: "Why, Mister Alden! Well? Will ye help my uncle's servant take my things up to the captain's cabin?"

Priscilla turned back in time to see Alden smiling and following Desire toward the companionway. Her skirts brushed the sailors, Shipley and Squint, working on a capstan.

"This may not be such a bad crossin' after all," Priscilla

heard Squint say as he held out his pants with a curtsey be-hind Desire's back.

Priscilla had seen one or two girls behave in Desire's fash-ion when she'd visited her aunt in London, but none quite so forward. Her father's sister was not a member of the Separat-ists, and her mother did not approve of the aunt's manner of living. Her father, however, wanted Priscilla's company when he had gone north from their farm in Surrey to Scrooby Manor to meet with his friends, William Brewster and Wil-liam Bradford.

It was at one of her aunt's parties that Priscilla had met David Kimberly, second son of an earl. Although David could not inherit the earl's estate, his father's influence had helped David obtain a prominent position with the govern-ment. He had pursued Priscilla eagerly and asked her to marry him several times, but handsome as he was, she finally came to realize that his gambling and flamboyant way of life would not suit her. So she had rejected him as she had re-jected Evan Smith, the son of a nearby farmer and a boy her father had wanted her to marry. But Evan was, while decent and hard-working, a very dull fellow. At eighteen, she felt cer-tain she would always be a spinster, alone with her books and maybe some cats. Therefore, when the voyage to America be-came a reality, she welcomed it gladly, and was surprised to find in herself a keen desire for adventure and for a real Chris-tian cause.

As she walked toward the companionway, she met her mother coming on deck. They joined her father and Joseph and the other passengers at the rail.

"Let us take one last, long look at our England," her father said, pulling Joseph to him.

They gazed out at the busy, picturesque port, with the fa-miliar houses, people, and ways of life. Priscilla noticed that her mother, who was almost always composed, had tears in her eyes. Priscilla gripped the rail tightly. Her father moved closer and put his arms around them both.

The confusion on the wharf was diminishing, and the on-lookers were starting to gather at the end of the dock.

"When are we going to go?" Joseph asked, fidgeting.

"Watch now, the ship will be getting under way," his father told him.

Just then the captain's voice boomed out across the ship. "Prepare to raise sail! All hands!"

The first mate echoed. "Prepare to raise sail! All hands!"

"Scramble ye bloody gobbets!" Jones bellowed. "Man that winch there! Hoist the tops'l! Hoist the mizzen!"

"Hoist the tops'l! Hoist the mizzen!" Clarke repeated.

"Raise anchor!"

The orders echoed down the ship. Suddenly the deck was swarming with sailors, rushing about. Some were hauling on the sheets as the sails started to unfold. The chains on the gangplank screeched as the anchor was drawn up. The winch for the mains'l began to turn, manned by two powerful men.

Orders continued to be shouted as the vessel strained at her hawsers.

"Let go the springline!"

"Let go the bowline!"

"Let go the sternline!"

"Raise the sheets!" the captain commanded.

The two enormous gray-white sails of the fore and aft main course began to rise and spread. The main tops'l and the fore tops'l unfurled, and finally the spanker and sprits'l were in place, like six large clouds overhead dwarfing the ship and men and the chaotic scene below.

The *Mayflower* heeled sharply over as the wind took her, slipped sideways from her moorings, shuddered, making the passengers gasp, then righted herself, the hull seeming to come alive as she plunged into the waves.

Priscilla caught sight of Dorothy Bradford standing rigidly at the rail, her husband's arm around her.

A sailor behind them was chasing John and Francis Billington.

The *Mayflower* made headway into the Sound between the Plym and Tamar Rivers and soon left the town and the towers of the old Tudor castle, guarding it, behind. Priscilla felt a tearing at her heart as she watched the receding gray shoreline.

Chapter Three

Once out in the channel, there was a sudden quiet on deck. The ship plowed steadily through small waves, powered by the light wind. The Billington boys still chased each other, but the sailors went about their business without speaking. The voyagers lowered their voices, as if the vessel, with its protective sails above, were some kind of cathedral, and they had just attended a sacred rite.

In twos and threes they drifted toward the hatch and went below decks. Alice soon left, followed by Joseph. After a moment Priscilla's father said: "I must help Mother. Will thee come soon?"

"Yes, soon" Priscilla answered, wanting to savor this strange time of both sadness and exhilaration.

In the distance she could see land as the sky cleared and the sun brightened. She stood, mesmerized, leaning over the rail, watching sparklets flicker on the water. Then, with a sigh, she turned and went below.

It was a far different situation that greeted her as she descended the steps of the companionway. People were struggling with their belongings, trying to set up some sort of order in the small spaces allotted them. There was noise everywhere, families calling to each other, children running and jumping about, their mothers shouting at them.

Everyone was swaying back and forth, rising up and down with the motion of the ship, like some crazy kaleidoscope. Priscilla saw her mother bending over, trying to find places for valises, trunks, crates, boxes, and sleeping pallets. When she saw Priscilla, she straightened up, her face red with exertion.

" 'Tis a bit of thy help we could use," she commented, handing Priscilla a blanket and a long cord. "And Mister Mullins," she added, "thee may take this bucket and fetch our allotment of water."

Mullins took the bucket and went topside.

Priscilla reached for the cord, weaving back and forth with the slant of the deck. "What be this for?" she asked.

"We will all need some privacy, both for ourselves and the families next to us. Stretch the cord and tie it securely around that beam. Then we will hang this blanket on it." She glanced up to see the Bradfords standing at the top of the companionway. She motioned to a stack of luggage and crates near them. "The Bradfords will be next to us. Poor Dorothy! I feel she will not enjoy this voyage."

They watched as the couple descended the stairs. Bradford was holding his wife's hand and helping her.

Priscilla remembered she had been visiting in Amsterdam at the time of the Bradfords' wedding. She had been thirteen then and Dorothy May sixteen. The young bride was the daughter of one of the leading Separatists and William the son of one of King James's Royal Guards. He had lost his father early but had inherited enough money for an education. Priscilla's mother told her that he had already learned to speak French, Latin, and a little Greek. While exiled in Holland, he had also taught himself to speak Dutch and had become a successful weaver of fustian cloth.

As they approached, Priscilla thought she had never seen a more handsome couple. He was a little above medium height, with strong, refined features and an air of splendid authority. Still he seemed tender and gentle, especially with Dorothy.

She was small, with skin as delicate as clouds tinted by the setting sun. She wore her black hair parted in the middle and drawn straight back to a coil on her neck, giving a simple frame to her exquisite face. Leaning on her husband's arm, with her dainty feet reaching out carefully under her brown woolen skirt, she looked very fragile. As she greeted the Mullins family, her face was quite without expression.

"Can I help thee get settled?" Alice offered.

"No, thank thee much," Dorothy replied distractedly.

"Well, let us know if ye need anything," Alice said with a glance at Bradford.

When William Mullins returned with the water, he and Priscilla and Joseph busied themselves following Alice's instructions. Other blankets were hung, giving an enclosed feeling to their space.

"Thee may put the cabinet and that trunk along this side if Joseph sleeps across the bottom at our feet."

Mullins considered the tiny spot. "Priscilla may go to the captain's cabin, if she wishes," he spoke hesitantly. " 'Twould relieve some of the crowding in this cubicle we have been given."

Alice's head jerked up. "So the captain said," she answered noncommittally.

Priscilla looked around, a clothespin in her mouth. She studied her parents a moment. "It would be nice to be with the other young ladies. And it would give thee some room. . . ."

"Yes, I know." Alice's back stiffened.

Mullins put his arm around her shoulders. "Priscilla must learn to stand by herself. 'Twould be a good experience for her."

"Humph! And what kind of an *experience?*"

"It is not as if she were some great distance away."

"I will be with thee most of the day . . . and I am eighteen years old!" Priscilla spoke firmly, shaking out a blanket.

"It is not the *day* I'm thinking of," her mother sighed.

"Mama!" Priscilla said, flushing, "I only want the company of the other young ladies, and Constance Hopkins and Elizabeth Tilley will be there, and they are younger than I am."

"Well, then," Alice spoke resignedly, wiping her brow with the back of her hand, "get thy things and thy papa will help thee get them above, and thee may stay if the other two girls be there, but come back here tonight." Priscilla smiled and hugged her mother.

Alice stopped her unpacking and watched as her daughter gathered her luggage, and, with her father, disappeared. Then, after another sigh, she said, putting her arm around her son: "Joseph, help me unroll these sleeping pallets."

When Priscilla and her father opened the door into the captain's cabin, they were surprised to find it already crowded, also. Besides twenty-year-old Desire Minter, with whom Priscilla had become slightly acquainted since leaving Southampton, there were also Elizabeth Tilley, Mary Chilton, and Constance Hopkins, girls of fourteen and fifteen, whom Priscilla had also met on shipboard. In addition, two small girls were standing in the middle of the room, heads down and a little frightened.

"Missus Carver and the captain brought them here," Constance Hopkins said, stepping over the valises and sleeping pallets on the floor.

"I guess it's all right," Desire added, turning around as she was hanging one of her dresses in the captain's wardrobe, "but I thought this cabin was to be entirely for young ladies."

Priscilla looked around to find a place for her father to put her trunk. The floor was covered with sleeping pallets, traveling cases, clothes, and trunks of the other girls who were busy arranging their belongings on the captain's chart table and chairs. Priscilla had never seen her father look so perplexed before, standing there helplessly as he glanced around.

"Here," Elizabeth Tilley offered, "we'll all move over. There's room."

The girls managed to leave a small corner vacant. Still there was no room for Priscilla's pallet. The girls look at each other hopelessly.

"Perhaps they can rig a hammock," Priscilla's father offered. "Most of the sailors use them."

"Oh, that would be jolly," Elizabeth laughed.

"I can see her swinging there." Desire gave an amused look.

"I will take it, if thee does not want it, Priscilla," Constance added.

"We can see about it in the morning," her father said nervously to Priscilla. "Thee can come below with us later on then, tonight." Mullins deposited the trunk among the petticoats and skirts and departed hastily.

As Priscilla started to settle herself, Mrs. Carver walked in with the small girls' belongings. "Desire, my dear," she said to her niece, "I thought the little girls would be better off here, since thee won't mind taking care of them."

Desire looked around slowly, her arms still on the clothes rack.

"They are orphans, ye know," the governor's wife said, addressing the other girls. "This one is Humility Cooper, and this is Ellen More. They are both eight years old, and Ellen has two little brothers aboard!" She smiled and kissed the children. "Now where will they sleep?" She looked about. "Here . . . here is a cozy place." She cleared the books from the captain's desk and stacked them on top of the bookshelves. Unrolling their small pallets, she tucked them in the corners of the desk top, which was enclosed on three sides. "There! That's a fine bed for the little ones. I know ye older girls will take good care of them." She smiled breezily and waved as she left.

"I don't know why *I* should take care of them!" Desire exclaimed. "They are wards of the church, and it was *thy* mother who wanted to bring them!" She pointed at Constance Hopkins.

Constance was a pretty girl, plump, with a jolly round face. "They are good girls," she replied, putting her hand on Humility's shoulder, "and not as lucky in being orphans as thee . . . Desire Minter."

Desire turned on her with a flushed face. "I am not exactly an orphan!" she exclaimed. "My parents were distant relatives of the Carvers, and, when my mama and papa died of the plague, the Carvers *begged* me to come live with them. My papa left me a large legacy which I will receive next year when I become twenty-one."

"That is, indeed, lovely," Constance answered, unruffled, as she began helping the little girls with their clothes.

Her unimpressed attitude further aggravated Desire. "And as to the care of the children, ye certainly should be accustomed to it, having no mother of thine own with a little brother and sister to care for, and thy father's new wife big with child already."

Constance made no answer. She turned her back, hiding her face.

Just then there was a knock on the door, and Priscilla and Elizabeth Tilley hurried to answer, thankful for the interruption.

There stood the captain and the ship's cook, with platters full of hot breads, mutton, leeks, and fresh fruit. Behind them stood John Alden with a large table. The captain hesitated, when he saw the disarray in his cabin, but then stepped stoically in as the girls hastened to clear a space for the victuals.

"It looks like a banquet!" Desire cried out, seeming to have regained her composure.

The captain looked at them amiably. "Ye will all be my daughters," he stated in a fatherly fashion, "for I have only two boys and have always wished for some girls."

Elizabeth and Constance hurried to make room on the chart table for the food. Everyone crowded around the cook and the captain with thanks, while the captain beamed, gratified and blissful. Then he remembered Alden.

"Here," he motioned for John to enter. "I've had Alden bring ye a table for your . . . ah . . . things." He looked around for a place to put it.

"Oh, right here, Mister Alden," Desire said, sweeping up the little girls' blankets, petticoats, shoes, and other personal effects from the floor that they had carefully unpacked. She gave him a sweet smile and stood back as Alden and the captain brought the table into the room. As Alden backed up, one of the table legs caught on the lace of a bodice, nearly tripping him. He started to fall backwards, and Priscilla hurriedly bent down and untangled the lace.

"Many thanks to ye," Alden said to her as she stood holding the undergarment.

Priscilla felt her face flush, and she hastily looked around for a place to put the bodice and, not finding one, dropped it by her feet as everyone watched.

"Well, good evening, ladies," the captain said. "Enjoy your supper." He left then with the cook and Alden following. As he closed the door, Priscilla saw Alden look at her, and she was almost sure she saw him wink. Then she quickly turned her attention back to her cabin mates and the food.

Priscilla took her plate and sat on the pallets, eating with the others. After arranging her effects as best she could, she reluctantly bade her cabin mates good evening with a longing backward glance.

In the cabin below decks, she found the uproar steadily increasing as the night wore on. The passengers were not allowed to cook this first night out, and families struggled to find some food and drink among the jumble of their belongings. Joseph became restless and hungry. The small children started crying while the older ones chased each other among people and possessions in the close quarters, increasing the din and tension.

The companionway was busy with people going above decks for fresh air as seasickness began to affect them. The Mullins family recoiled as someone fell against one of their blankets. Alice shook her head in dismay.

"Here," she said to her family, "enjoy this fresh beef and milk left over from the inn, while ye can. It may be cold but 'twill be the last ye may have for a while. Joseph, take this bowl to Carter. Priscilla, I know ye have eaten, but a bite more won't hurt. Ye are too thin."

"Remember," the mate called out as he started up the companionway after his nightly check, "only six lighted lanterns allowed in this cabin. Too much danger of fire. Mind what I say!"

After they had eaten, Mullins took out his Bible, and the four of them held hands. "Bless this journey, O Lord, we pray, that we may arrive safely at our destination. And bless our daughter, too, that the lessons she learns while being separated from us may be to Thy greater glory. 'Lead us not into temptation, but deliver us from evil,' we earnestly beseech Thee, 'for Thine is the kingdom and the power and the glory forever.' Amen." Priscilla and her father exchanged knowing looks as he finished the prayer.

As the passengers prepared for sleep, the babel gradually subsided. There were murmurs and occasional low laughs as people realized the nearness of strangers. The ship swung back and forth, back and forth, with eerie creaking sounds, but sleep finally came, and the cabin grew quiet.

The mate slipped down the stairs again, snuffed out two more of the lanterns, leaving the passageway only dimly lighted. A little child whimpered in the dark, and then there was only the swish of waves washing the hull and the comforting regular sound of the ship's bells.

Priscilla turned over in her strange bed, thinking of the many events that had brought the family to this ship.

Chapter Four

William Mullins, tall, rugged but dignified—"descendent of the great French house of Anjou," as he liked to say—had been a successful shoemaker. He had also been a farmer by necessity since he needed to raise cattle for his shoe hides. He'd considered himself a practical man, a decent, hard-working fellow who cared properly for his loved ones, his work, his body, and his Bible. He had overcome early poverty, was not wealthy but thriving, had a loving family, and a good trade. However, he had not been satisfied.

"A man should have freedom from the restricted class order, an opportunity to improve himself," he had often told his friends. "A man needs certain goals, something worth living for . . . even something worth dying for."

He had read every book he could come by, making trips thrice annually to the booksellers in Londontown from his farm near Dorking, Surrey, despite the dangers from highwaymen. He especially enjoyed the works of William Shakespeare, the popular playwright, and had visited the Globe theater three times before Shakespeare's death in 1616, four years before. Once, he liked to boast, he had even met John Shakespeare, William's father, a glove maker, when he had needed extra hides. The old man had been regretfully selling his farm, Ingon Meadow, at Sutterfield outside Stratford, and was complaining because his son had had no interest in the glove business.

On such trips to London, Mullins had often made the farther journey to Scrooby Manor to talk with his friend, William Brewster, who had been an assistant to the prime minister and was the agent in charge of the manor. At times, Mullins would hear a pastor, John Robinson, preach there. Those who gathered about Robinson were called Separatists because they wished to break with the Church of England. They denounced its strict canons and capricious courts where guilt or innocence was decided by the ability to pay and that the King ruled by self-declared divine right, as if he were a super-being. While the Puritans (a derisive name forced on them by their foes) had hoped to "purify" the English Church of Roman Catholicism, the Separatists wished only to return to the simple way of life of the 1st-Century Christians where the leader of each church would be answerable only to the members of its own congregation and not to the whims of a sovereign or a wider church clergy.

At Scrooby, Mullins had also met William Bradford, a young iconoclast, an interesting and stimulating young man, who was also an ardent Separatist. The religious meetings were, of course, forbidden by the King's edicts, and Mullins had became apprehensive as arrests of some of the Separatists were being made. It was rather daring, Mullins thought, that Robinson and Brewster, both educated at Cambridge University, were berating the Church of England in this place, for Scrooby Manor, that Brewster managed, was actually a hostelry for wealthy travelers and one of the manors of the Archbishop of York. It was possible that the Archbishop, a friend of Brewster's, if he knew of the meetings, simply ignored them, since the bishops of the church deeply resented the King's dictates to them.

These three men—William Mullins, William Brewster, and William Bradford—had had many discussions on the subjects of Robinson's sermons. Still, twelve years ago, when Brewster and many other Separatists had been imprisoned and then had sold their homes and farms to flee to Holland, Mullins had not been ready to go with them. He had been thirty years old at that time and Priscilla six. He was the owner of a small farm and cottage that had taken all his money and many hours of hard labor to develop, as he often reminded his family.

His trade, making shoes as his father had done, was then just starting to show a little profit. Too much time, money, and strength had been invested here in England to throw it all away and start over in a strange country where he did not even know the language. And so the family had remained in England. Six years later Joseph had been born.

The decision not to emigrate had not satisfied him. Life in England grew steadily worse. He felt that crime, robbery, bribery, and immorality were increasing all over the country. Even the bishop of their own church had been reprimanded and removed by the King's order for not demanding enough contributions for the royal coffers from the members of the province.

The Mullins family had gone to the Netherlands twice to visit Pastor Robinson, Elder Brewster, and the others, who were referred to as "Pilgrims" since their emigration to Holland. Priscilla's parents had been much impressed with the exiles' adjustment, their courage, and unselfishness in their strange surroundings. They had worked and saved their money for twelve years for a vision—a vision of having a community free from outside influences and controls. Holland had not suited these needs.

William Bradford had sent a letter to Mullins. After he read it to himself, he read it aloud to Alice and Priscilla.

The twelve years of truce with Spain came to an end, and there was nothing but beating of drums and preparations for war. We lived in Holland but as men in exile. So we resolved with great hope and inward zeal, to leave Holland and find a place suitable for our work for the Lord and Jesus Christ.

"And they decided on America?" Alice asked.

"No. In the beginning they were quite divided," Mullins said, and went on reading.

There were many who chose Guyana because of its fertile soil and hot climate. And true it is that it is rich, fruitful, and blessed with a perpetual spring . . . and nature brings forth all things in abundance without much labor on the part of man. They argued that it must make the habitants rich, seeing that less clothing and provisions would serve. And the Spaniards, whose territory it is, already had more lands than they could rightly handle and would probably leave us alone.

"Guyana is in the southern hemisphere," Mullins interjected, "in South America."

This was agreed to, but then some felt they might have strange diseases there that colder climates are free from, and that the Spaniards might be jealous of our good fortune and drive us out as they had the French in Florida. We were guided by our pastor, John Robinson, whom ye knew, and Elder Brewster, and prayed much over this problem, and, at length, the conclusion was to live as a distinct body unto ourselves under the general government of the Virginia Company in America and to ask King James to grant us religious freedom. Two were then chosen to go to influential friends and beseech the King on this matter. The Virginia Company was very desirous that we settle there and would give us a patent, but the King would not grant us his seal for freedom of worship. However, he had indi-

cated that he would not molest us so far away. Then some added that, although we had a seal as broad as a house floor, it would not serve us, for there would be found means anew to recall or reverse it if the King so chose.

Thus it was decided we would rest on God's providence. We dispatched messengers, John Carver and Robert Cushman, to make the best arrangements with the Virginia Company that we could, and to procure a patent with as good and ample conditions as they might by any good means obtain.

"It seems they must have had high hopes for the Virginia Company. They should be glad to have settlers on their land," Alice commented.

Mullins continued reading.

At first all went well. We were promised whatever monies and provisions we should need. But ye do not know what transpired later. Thomas Weston, a London merchant known to us and seeming to befriend us, urged us to draw up some conditions and put up some of our money from our common stock, and he would represent us in obtaining the patent agreement. Thus the articles were drawn up in Leyden.

Meanwhile, we heard that certain lords had gotten a grant from the King for large areas north of the Virginia patent, and entirely secluded from the government that was to be called New England. There were some of us who then desired to change our plans and proceed there. Others were still protesting about Guyana.

Mullins paused and reflected. "Men are too prone to desire comfort," he commented, "not thinking clearly whether the change is for the better or the worse. It is the desire to gamble, I suppose." He then went on reading.

★ ★ ★ ★ ★

Those who had sold their homes and put up their money were fearful the whole plan would fall through, and we were well aware the summer was getting away from us! Finally the majority agreed on going to the land the Virginia Company owned!

"That must have been a great relief!" Priscilla remarked.
"Not for long," Mullins said.

The Virginia Company then decided to change some of the articles drawn up in Leyden, and incredibly Thomas Weston and Robert Cushman agreed and signed the contracts without even consulting us! This caused great trouble and contention, for one of the changes bound us to work for seven years before our shares in the corporation with the merchants would be given to us!

"Seven years. That's too long," Mullins commented, and then continued reading.

And furthermore, our children under sixteen are to have no shares granted but fifty acres of unmanured land! There are other changes we objected to also. But what could we do? It had been signed!

There was silence as Mullins put the letter down.

More and more, in the next few months, Priscilla's father had turned to his Bible. While trying to appear the same businessman, it was plain to see he was inwardly reaching.

" 'Ye shall seek Me and find Me when ye shall search for Me with all your heart,' " he had kept reading to the family.

41

There were those who claimed to have seen visions of being *called*. Mullins expected no such thing, nor did anything like that happen. Yet, one day they had noticed a certain strength in him, a relaxed power. He told them he had found faith. He now had a goal, he said, to try to make his own life an example of Jesus Christ's and of God's Word.

"For faith without works is dead," he said. "I now understand why my friends went to Holland."

Not only Mullins but some of their neighbors had been unhappy with the lack of regard for the straightforward teachings of Christ in the Church of England. There was more ritual and pageantry than emphasis on honesty, good will, and kindness in daily living. They had become increasingly irritated by the petulance and growing arrogance of the King and his summary edicts, forcing his people to acclaim his rights divine. It was a time of great sinfulness, violence, crime, and corruption.

Priscilla could see that her father was anxious to join Brewster, Bradford, and the others. Finally he had expressed his thoughts to his family.

"Good wife, if it be thy will as well as mine, let us go with these good people."

Priscilla knew her mother would agree, not only in deference to her husband, but, coming as she did from a family of fisherpeople, she was used to the sea and adventure. "Descendant of one of those Viking raids on England," her husband had often teased her. Priscilla was excited at the prospect, and Joseph was overjoyed.

"Thee knows it means leaving England, this farm, this house, this business, our family and friends . . . forever?"

Put that way it made Alice and Priscilla gasp. They looked at him, absorbing the prospect slowly.

Then Mullins said: "I feel it to be the Lord's guidance."

He had said this humbly, and, as Alice held out her hand, the matter was settled.

Even Robert Carter, the old man Mullins had hired five years ago to help work the farm, had wanted to go with them. Mullins had paid the passage for all five of them, at ten pounds per person.

Alice had immediately begun making preparations to leave. Certain pieces of furniture, their china and silver, and other family treasures were to go, for the family must maintain the graces and refinements of their present mode of living insofar as possible. Joseph nettled them constantly. Upon awakening in the morning, he would ask: "Are we going today?"

Then a letter came from William Brewster. He asked Mullins to introduce John Carver and a certain Robert Cushman to some marine investors in London with whom Mullins was acquainted, having sent shipments of shoes across the Channel to noblemen in France and Spain several times. The Separatists had saved enough money to purchase a small ship, the *Speedwell*, that would not only transport some of them to the New World but would serve for scouting, fishing, and trade when they arrived at their destination. They now wished to charter a larger ship for the rest of the emigrants. To accomplish this they needed further financing.

After several meetings, an agreement was drawn up, and the *Mayflower* was chosen for the trip.

Then another letter had arrived from Bradford in London, and again Mullins read it aloud to his family.

> *In the last three weeks we have made countless arrangements. We sold or packed all our goods. Everything was got in readiness. We then left from Delftshaven, a few miles from Leyden, on July 22nd. It was a sad farewell, for many of our*

friends stayed in Holland, and our beloved pastor, John Robinson, felt he must stay with them.

Mullins sighed. "That was a serious loss. He greatly desired to be with us."

He and many of our friends came from Amsterdam and Leyden to wish us Godspeed. We spent the night before with little sleep, but with friendly entertainment and talk and real expressions of true Christian love. The next day there was a sorrowful leave-taking and then the tide, which stays for no man, took us toward England.

Mullins folded the letter. "We must join them soon."

Finally the farm and livestock were sold, the packing finished, and the family departed for Southampton in a neighbor's wagon in the middle of the night.

The day the two ships, the *Mayflower* and the *Speedwell*, left Southampton had been bright and sunny—a day to remember. Flags and banners had dressed the rigging, with the Cross of St. George atop the highest mast. There were crowds and shouting and excitement everywhere, with horns blowing and drums beating as the ships left port. Spirits were high with anticipation of a fast and pleasant voyage. The Channel had been smooth, and there was very little seasickness.

It was on August 8th, the third day at sea, that the *Speedwell* began flying trouble flags. At noon she pulled close to the *Mayflower*. With his bullhorn Captain Reynolds informed Captain Jones that his ship was leaking and that he durst not go on. After further bellowing back and forth across the water, it was resolved that the two ships would put back into Dartmouth harbor.

When the passengers had expressed great disappointment, Elder Brewster had called them all together and calmed them saying: "It is the will of the Lord, and let us put our trust in Him."

Those quartered on the *Mayflower* remained there, but those on the *Speedwell* had been forced to find shelter ashore. The *Speedwell* had been searched for leaks and some weak spots found, but nothing serious. However, there had been heavy charges and port fees and the loss of over eight days.

At last the two ships put to sea again with high resolve and prayers that the voyage would be successful this time. Then three days out of Dartmouth another delay had befallen them. For the second time the ships had to put into port, this last time at Plymouth, again at the complaint of the *Speedwell*'s captain. He had maintained that the vessel was still leaking.

"No special leak could be found," William Bradford told the group at Plymouth, "but it was judged the general weakness of the ship that she would not be found sufficient for the voyage."

Some of the Separatists had felt that it was not so much the ship that was unseaworthy as her captain.

"And so," Bradford continued, "after we take out such provisions as the *Mayflower* can well stow, and conclude what number and what persons to send back, we shall make another sad parting. Those of our friends who are going back are, for the most part, willing to do so, either out of some discontent, or fear they conceived of the ill success of the voyage, seeing so many crosses befall and the year so far spent. Others have asked to go back either because of weakness or ill health or having many young children, unto which work of God and judgment of their brethren they were content to submit. And thus," Bradford sadly concluded, "like Gideon's army, our small number is divided, as if the Lord, by the work of His providence, thought these few too many for the great work He has to do."

"In place of those sent back," Mullins told Alice and Priscilla afterward, "we have to take many strangers aboard who have already paid independently and so will crowd our ship to congestion, and our Separatist group will be lessened to just forty-one adults and twelve children."

So it was that Priscilla and her British family, farmers and shoemakers, found themselves aboard a rocking ship, crowded in with over a hundred other people, headed across a vast ocean toward an alien land.

Chapter Five

Priscilla awakened early, after a restless and often sleepless night. She started when she saw the unfamiliar surroundings in the dim light. Then she remembered where she was. The air was fresh, with that singular smell of the sea, and beckoned her outside.

She slipped silently into her dress and, leaving her family sleeping soundly, quietly went up to the main deck. It was very early, but already several women were preparing food. The first mate had arranged the passengers into shifts for cooking.

The sun-speckled sea, the soft breeze, and the scent of the morning meal being prepared on the sand-based fire boxes distracted her thoughts, and she stared out over the water, missing the sight of the *Speedwell*, sailing alongside them. Still half asleep, she leaned on the rail, hypnotized by the passing wavelets. Suddenly she became aware of John Alden, standing alongside her.

"Casts a spell over ye, doesn't it?" he said softly, looking down at the water. "And ye never tire of it on a day like this."

"How long have ye been a sailor?" she asked curiously.

"Oh, six or seven years, I guess. Ever since I was a lad."

"Don't ye miss the land?"

"That I do . . . and take some months off now and again and do some carpentry ashore. I came to ask ye when I can hang your hammock."

"Oh, yes, well," she thought for a minute, "whenever it's convenient for the other girls."

"Perhaps about ten o'clock. It seems there are requests for three more of them now. I'll need room to work and maybe the place cleared a bit, if ye don't mind."

"That will be fine. I'll ask them to clear a place."

"All right, then," he said, and went off whistling.

Presently Priscilla's father joined her, and then William Brewster and Governor Carver came along. After greetings, they, too, became silent, watching the shore receding in the distance.

"That's Land's End out there," Brewster murmured. " 'Tis bittersweet, seeing the last of England."

"Let us hope this time we have!" Carver spoke.

War whoops interrupted him as John and Francis Billington accompanied by Joseph Mullins and Bartholomew Allerton chased each other around the deck until Francis, tripping on a sail, fell hard against the sailor Shipley's shoulder.

"Ye brats!" the man exclaimed, giving Francis a slap. He then started after all of them. Alice Mullins, coming from below decks, stepped out to catch Joseph, but her husband held her back. "He must learn," Mullins said.

Joseph was a ragamuffin of a boy, enjoying life with the zest of a seven-month-old puppy, but sensitive, not only to his own feelings but for others, also. With Mullins, Alice, and Priscilla watching, Joseph pulled Bartholomew Allerton down behind a cannon as Shipley rushed by after Francis. When Shipley caught Francis by the shirt tail and began walloping him, Joseph jumped out, followed by Bartholomew Allerton, and they were joined by John Billington. They all went after Shipley.

Francis set up a terrible howl, echoed immediately by John. Soon all four boys were yelling and jumping on Shipley.

From the poop deck came the captain's shout. "By the

black devil himself! What's going on? Clarke, grab those boys! Where's their mother?" He roared: "*Missus* Billington!"

Mrs. Billington came forward from her cook pot with a sigh. "John! . . . Francis! Come 'ere this minute!" She chased after her boys, catching them by their shirts. " 'Ave ye been mischiefing these men?"

Joseph, followed by Bartholomew, came and stood by his parents.

"We weren't hurting anything, Maw," Francis screamed, and Joseph suddenly stepped forward. "Just playing tag, sir," he said to the captain in a small voice.

"Well," the captain said as he leaned over the rail, "ye'll have to keep your young 'uns out of trouble. Keep those urchins below, if they can't keep out of the way."

"Get below! I'll see ye later!" Mullins ordered Joseph and Bartholomew, and they walked slowly and stiffly away, heads down.

Mrs. Billington looked up at the captain and whined: " 'Tis me spends every wakin' hour tryin' t' control 'em. What can a poor woman do when 'er good man never lifts a 'and t' help 'er?" She caught sight of her husband, emerging from the hatch. "John Billington!" she called to him over the heads of the sixty or more people cooking and eating. "Mind your boys!"

"Take it smooth, woman," the man said, lumbering up to her. "What's it now?" He motioned to the boys to leave. While he remonstrated with the captain, the boys disappeared into a small tool house.

"The children got *some* rights," Billington was saying, ". . . an' kids need to *play!*"

Suddenly the captain looked up and gasped. Francis, having found a musket, was trying to lift and fire it.

"Watch out!" the captain shouted and cringed back.

There followed a loud blast, and a wooden barrel rocked back and forth. Everyone stood as if transfixed. Then the captain, teeth clenched, spoke in a steadily rising voice.

"See that big keg over there ye just missed . . . that's gunpowder . . . enough to blow us all to hell!"

An uproar broke out. Women screamed. Men shouted. Shipley grabbed his chest, pretended to faint. "I quit!" he announced.

Brewster stepped up one or two steps on the ladder and lifted an arm for silence.

"*Quiet*, brethren."

All the passengers, strangers and churchmen alike, turned toward him.

"Gunpowder. And by the Lord's grace he missed. Let us not be alarmed but remain calm. There has been no harm done, but Mister Billington . . . take your boys in hand and see that they are properly disciplined."

Priscilla saw her father smile. "See how quickly the elder stepped up to save the boys from the captain's wrath," he whispered to her, "and already the strangers have accepted his leadership."

As the boys were escorted across the deck, John deliberately pushed against Shipley, who turned on him. "Get below, ye stinks . . . or I'll feed ye to the fishes!" He made a threatening move toward them with a belaying pin he grabbed off the bulkhead. The boys dodged behind their mother.

"Don't ye dare lay a hand on my boys! John! Protect your family!"

Billington simpered at the sailor. "They don't mean it bad. They're just kids, y' know."

Captain Jones suddenly appeared right behind them. "Get those *brats* below." The boys looked up at the captain's red face and ran for the companionway.

Dorothy Bradford stepped up to her husband who was watching the scene along with everyone else. "William, don't let that evil sailor hurt them. They're just not used to being so confined. Our little boy looks a little like the younger one."

Mrs. Billington saw them watching her. "Prithee, do ye 'ave children?"

"One little son. We felt we should leave him with my mother. He's only five years old, and he was ill. We didn't feel the New World would be a good place for him for a while."

Mrs. Billington took it as an affront. "Well! Leavin' your own. Me an' me good man could do no such thing." She turned away with a clucking sound.

Bradford hastened to intervene. "She really didn't intend to be unkind. It's just her way."

Dorothy Bradford stepped back, paused, then left the deck hurriedly, followed by her husband.

Priscilla and Alice, who had started to leave, could not help seeing the anguished look on Dorothy Bradford's face.

Mullins stepped up to Mrs. Billington. "That was very thoughtless, my dear woman. Missus Bradford had her reasons. You must remember that our ship is small, and there are many souls living together here for who knows for how long. We *must* be thoughtful and kind to each other, or we are lost."

"Well," Mrs. Billington snorted, "I don't notice anyone bein' kind and thoughtful t' *me*."

Shipley stepped up to her. "We're doin' our best, yer grace," he sneered.

As things began to quiet down, the women started back to their cooking. Priscilla went below to fetch the pot and ingredients for the family breakfast. It was difficult getting the iron container to hang evenly, for the tripod did not set firmly as it should. Eventually the porridge was heated, and Priscilla carried it to the family cubicle while Alice gathered the family. After prayers and breakfast, Priscilla excused herself and went up to the captain's cabin.

She was alone when Alden knocked on the door, the other girls still below decks with their families. She offered to move their possessions aside so Alden could work. "I'll call the other girls."

"No need of that. Now where is it ye want *your* hammock hung?" he said. "We'll start with that."

Alden did not seem in any way annoyed by all the feminine paraphernalia as they moved things about, but made fun of it, putting on one of the bonnets and tying on a ruffled apron. "Now, ye see, I'm ready for work," he said soberly.

Priscilla did not know just what he would do next, so she gave him a small condescending smile.

"Now I will teach thee how to put bolts in a beam," he said, using the intimate word to address her as he removed the bonnet and apron. "Here, thee may pass me these," and he handed her the bolts as he climbed the ladder with his tools. Once, when she held up the bolt, his hand grasped hers as he reached around without looking down. She told herself it was only an accident.

"Well," he said, when her hammock was hung, "let's see thee try it."

Priscilla declined, but he insisted. "I must set it at the right height for thee. 'Tis easy," he said, sitting on it and swinging his feet around to lie down. "Come now." He jumped off and took her hand to guide her.

Priscilla gingerly sat on the edge of the hammock and, holding her skirts tightly around her legs, tried to swing them up and in. Suddenly the hammock turned completely over, and she would have been flipped to the floor except for Alden's catching her.

"That's not the way thee must do it," he said, letting her go immediately. His face was very straight, but she suspected he had known very well what would happen. "There's a trick to it," he laughed. "Try again."

Priscilla, straightening her gown and feeling her face flush, told him it was nearly time for her to report to the main deck. She tried to walk sedately out the door, leaving him to finish alone. For such a quiet, rather shy person before others, he was quite a forward one alone, she thought. She did not dislike him exactly, but she certainly did not approve.

To keep the young children occupied, the governor had asked his wife Catherine, Mary Brewster, Alice Mullins, Priscilla, and Desire Minter to organize classes five days a week. Some were to be by ages, some by sexes. Elder Brewster taught two Bible study classes, one for the older children, one for the younger. Mary Brewster, Alice Mullins, Mary Chilton, and Priscilla were in charge of hymn singing. Desire and Constance Hopkins taught art and sewing to the older girls as both were known for their fine needlepoint.

Priscilla, assisted by Elizabeth Tilley, also taught a story-telling class for the little ones. This was Priscilla's favorite for she loved to watch the children's expressions as they reacted to her fables and rhymes.

Reporting for the singing were bright, little, five-year-old Resolved White with his sandy hair and eager look; tiny four-year-old Mary Allerton and her six-year-old sister, Remember, who had blonde hair and dark eyes like Priscilla's; Henry Sampson, an alert and self-confident six-year-old; three-year-old Damaris Hopkins, curly-haired with an ever-present bewitching smile; smart John Crackston; and John Billington, who paid very little attention; three six-year-olds—Samuel Fuller, the doctor's son, Wrassle

Brewster, who tried to live up to his name, wiggling and squirming through every story and teasing the other children, and Priscilla's brother, Joseph, who took special delight in being a party to any mischief in progress. Then there were the three orphans, Jasper and Richard More, six and seven respectively, and their sister Ellen who was eight and belonged with the older group, but who had cried when separated from her little brothers. Sometimes the class sat spellbound for one of Priscilla's stories; and sometimes, to her and Elizabeth's dismay, the children became noisy and roguish.

Priscilla and Elizabeth stayed to watch the next class. Governor Carver had asked the captain to spare Alden to teach the boys the art of carpentry and barrel-making, and several of the fathers also came to watch the demonstrations, bearing in mind their need for this craft in the new country.

The day was a busy one for during the older children's Bible lesson Priscilla and Elizabeth Tilley were asked to assist Elder Brewster. He took his seat on a large crate with the children sitting cross-legged around him. Priscilla and Elizabeth counted—to be sure all seventeen of the children between six and twelve years old were present.

"And where is Master Jasper More?" Priscilla asked of Richard, his brother.

"He's sick," Richard answered. "And the doctor says he's to stay abed." He made it sound very important.

"We wish him well," Elder Brewster answered, "and you send him our good wishes and our *love*. And that is the subject for our lesson today. It is from a letter . . . a letter from Saint Paul to his friends in a city called Corinth. He tells them and us, too, that we must love and care about each other, and that is the commandment of Jesus Christ."

The elder went on teaching as the children listened to his

deep, soft voice. As he read, Priscilla noticed that John Alden had come on deck and was leaning back against the rail, a long, round piece of polished wood in his hand. It looked something like a flute. When the lesson was finished, Elder Brewster motioned to John to come forward.

"Mister Alden has a surprise for ye," he announced. "Do thee remember how the shepherds played their pipes and sang while they watched their sheep the night Jesus was born? Well, Mister Alden has made a shepherd's pipe like that, and he is going to play it for ye."

The children were delighted and sat in awe as the first clear notes came forth. Alden stopped a moment and adjusted his fingers on the pipe. Then he played a merry roundelay for them to sing. Following that came a soft, plaintive aria, the sweet sounds floating like birds on the warm breeze. The melody, the rhythm of the waves, and the hypnotic swaying of the boat lulled Priscilla into an aura of tranquillity. She turned toward the musician and saw with surprise that Alden was watching her.

The day passed swiftly what with trying to bring order to the captain's cabin and then trying to help her mother to better arrange food, dishes, clothing, cooking utensils, blankets, trunks, books, and other necessities in their cramped quarters. Soon it was their turn to go above and cook supper. Alice debated whether or not to try fixing a chicken but decided to settle for pea soup with a few pieces of salt pork in it and the few remaining carrots from their former garden.

Priscilla took Alice to show her the captain's cabin after evening prayers were said on the main deck. Her mother caught the happy mood of the girls' voices and laughter.

"Sometimes we wore *wooden shoes!*" Mary Chilton was saying.

"In Holland, in the spring, whenever it rains, the sea runs

over the land, and the streets and ground are always wet," Elizabeth Tilley added.

"Didn't the shoes hurt?" Desire asked.

"Oh, certainly, at first. But we soon became accustomed to them. They were rather fun. Everyone clopped along like horses on the cobblestones."

After Alice left, the girls started preparing for sleep. It was long past midnight, after the laughter had turned to quiet talk and the quiet talk to whispers, before Priscilla felt herself being rocked to sleep by the swinging of the hammock and the lullaby of the wind, sighing through the sails.

Chapter Six

The prosperous winds continued, and the ship's company settled into a routine. The sails were plump as pillows, and the bow sliced smoothly through the water. Most of the passengers had recovered from their seasickness, and there was less grumbling over the crowded quarters. The cubicles in the main cabin, although much too small, had been arranged in the fairest and most efficient manner possible.

Eating was the principal problem, for food had to be carefully rationed, storage and cooking were difficult, and there was no room for tables on which to eat. There was a shortage of water for drinking and very little for washing. Consequently the ship's company was forced to drink wine or beer with their meals and to go with only wet cloths for wiping faces and hands. The beer was mild, however, and the Separatists who had lived in Holland had become quite used to it since the water there had been impure. Many hammocks had been hung for sleeping in the main cabin, providing extra space, and, aside from children crying, Priscilla's parents reported that the hours of rest were fairly well respected.

Prayer meetings were held on the main deck every morning and evening with all the passengers and crew welcome. Many of the strangers (those who were not Separatists) attended, some glad of relief from the monotony, some curious, and some with genuine interest. The sailors, however, scoffed at the worshippers but were restrained somewhat by the captain.

One morning, after hymn singing, most of the girls went

up to the captain's cabin. Priscilla and Constance Hopkins brought their sewing outside on the upper deck and sat on barrels to work. Below them, several sailors were gathered together, mending sail. They were watching as the last of the singers disappeared below, unaware of the two above them.

Jyp, sitting back against a crate on his haunches, got up and looked down into the main cabin. "They're packed in there like cod in a barrel!" he said.

"They're 'exed, y' know," Squint told the others. "Think all they 'ave t' do is sit around prayin' an' singin' an' the Lord'll take care o' 'em." He kneeled, hands folded, and rolled his eyes about.

Priscilla and Constance looked at each other and covered their mouths to keep from laughing.

"Ye watch," Shipley sneered, "they'll sing. We'll do the work. Lost me limey buttons, I 'ave, signin' on for this sailin' with these abbey lubbers aboard!"

Jyp sat down and went back to work. "Wait'll they get t' nowheres land at the mouth o' the 'Udson . . . with snow piled fifty feet 'igh. They'll work!"

"Aye, an' not a friendly face t' see . . . just 'eathen savages, ready t' cut their 'earts out an' serve 'em up for tea . . . eh, Coppin? Ye've been there."

Priscilla saw Constance raise her eyebrows with a shiver.

"That's so," Coppin, the second mate, replied. "I was there with Cap'n Smith. There's mostly aught but them redskins . . . a 'oopin and a 'ollerin' around till ye think yer in 'ell fer sure! I told ye that's all I saw when I made me last voyage across . . . but then, I guess the land could be all right fer farmin'."

" 'Tis worth it, though," Squint nodded wisely, "if they really be rubies an' emeralds lyin' around fer ye t' pick up easy-like."

Constance raised her eyebrows again at Priscilla, this time with a wide grin.

Coppin shrugged. "I saw no rubies nor emeralds neither, but then we didn't get too far north, an' there are them as do say that's where they be."

"Still an' all, this be no trip fer them as likes their comforts," Shipley smirked, "an' from all I see, these abbey lubbers likes it plenty." He leaned toward Squint. "Let's rough 'em up a bit."

"None o' yer mischief, Shipley," Coppin warned. "These folk paid their passage, an' the captain is t' deliver 'em 'ealthy." With that he rose and left.

The girls quietly slipped back into the cabin where they burst out with muffled laughter. Then Priscilla put her finger to her lips. "Not a word," she whispered. "We shouldn't have been listening. It's not right."

That afternoon Priscilla noticed her father on deck, standing alone at the rail. The sea had become choppy, and the sun glided in and out of the dark clouds like a child playing hide-and-seek. The breeze was suddenly cooler.

"It feels as if autumn is coming," Priscilla said, stepping up beside her father.

Mullins looked around. "Thee startled me."

Priscilla laughed and took his arm. "How long has thee been here?"

"Oh, a while," he answered. "I came after the governor's meeting. And where is thy mother? And Joseph? I thought he'd be playing on deck."

"They're below, I'm sorry to say," she answered, "with a touch of seasickness."

"Ah, poor woman, this is the way of it, Viking blood or not. And Joseph, too? We'd best go down and see to them in a bit. And thee, Priscilla?" He looked at her quizzically. "How does it go in the cabin above?"

"Oh, very well, indeed." There was a glint in her eyes, and she almost winked at him. He patted her hand, and she put hers on his arm, and she felt happy with their close kinship.

Governor Carver, William Brewster, and William Bradford joined them, conversing excitedly, obviously having come from the same meeting.

"To think of the useless time we've lost over that ship, the *Speedwell* . . . what a noxious name," Bradford said.

"Here it is nearing October already," Carver admitted. "And we had thought to make the voyage with some order, some regard for our funds, and some regard for the seasons."

Then Richard Warren, Isaac Allerton, and Edward Winslow, young men of about thirty, joined the group.

"Now there are just too many of us crowded into that cabin below," Winslow was commenting, "and I fear for our sanity, stuffed in there like seeds in a bin . . . and there are twenty-four single men aboard with only five single young women, and the three of them less than fifteen years old." He seemed embarrassed as Priscilla and her father turned around.

Priscilla felt her face flush. Just then Isaac Allerton broke in with a loud voice: "That captain was a bloody coward. He has cost us all our remaining capital and many of our provisions."

"Softly, Allerton," Brewster said, "we are *gentle* men."

"And did ye know that our esteemed treasurer, Christopher Martin," Warren went on, "signed a contract with the London merchants that we must work *seven* days a week for them until our debt for this voyage is paid off?" He spoke with exasperation. "That will take *years!*"

"We must work on the Sabbath?" Brewster disapproved.

"That's in the contract . . . that's what I heard," Winslow said, "and, furthermore, Martin even refuses to show us his accounts."

"Yes, I'm afraid that's the contract Martin signed," Mullins was forced to agree, "and without the governor's approval."

"He's right," Carver agreed. "While we were in Holland, he and Thomas Weston signed many papers without our approval. And at the end of that time of servitude the merchant lenders say we will have to forfeit our *houses*, although we have signed no such agreement."

"That cannot be," Bradford stated flatly. "Our houses, when we get them, *must* belong to us."

"Yes, it's been a difficult time financially," Carver affirmed.

"And when we arrive," Winslow groaned, "it may be winter and no shelter . . . and a wilderness full of savages. I honestly fear for our survival."

Mullins pulled away from them and looked across the sea. "We may be sorely tried, but we should have no fear. For 'if ye dwell in the uttermost parts of the sea, even there will His hand hold us.' "

Brewster nodded. "The Israelites must have had much more anxiety when Moses led them into the wilderness with no foreseeable haven."

"But they didn't have to sign a contract, saying they would work for seven days a week for *years!*" Warren protested.

"No, Richard," Brewster replied, "but they wandered forty years in the desert. Would ye prefer that?"

Warren smiled. "Ye are right. We must count our blessings."

Bradford added: "I'll confess now that many a time I felt we were making a mistake . . . leaving our warm homes in Holland."

John Langemore, Christopher Martin's boundman, turned toward them from a group of newcomers who had boarded at Plymouth and was now standing around one of the cooking fires. He was a pinch-faced, rough-looking man, about twenty-five. "Mark ye now, if ye were so comfortable, why then did ye leave Holland? This be no milk and honey spot we're headed for."

"No," Bradford added quickly, "but Holland was about to be forced into war with Spain . . . and we don't believe in war."

"Wars only lead to more wars until the whole world will be destroyed," Brewster declared. "We must work toward more understanding among all the people of the earth. We believe that working together with the practice of love and kindness and less personal greed can bring mankind joy and peace in place of destruction. We will follow the Christian precept."

"We could not return to England," Carver informed Langemore and the others who had gathered around him. "There are no morals. There is drunkenness everywhere, and the streets and highways are not safe from the criminals who get their freedom easily from the lax courts. And the King believes us to be some threat to his church. At the Hampton Court conference he threatened *all* who do not worship as he dictates. Many of us have been imprisoned and have a price on our heads. We desire decent, righteous lives for ourselves and for our children, and for these simple views we are harassed."

"Ye see, Langemore," Brewster explained more calmly, "in this New World we will actually be *free* men . . . united in the common good as we all should be."

"I know ye are not one of us," Priscilla's father said earnestly to Langemore, "but I hope ye understand what we are striving for."

" 'Tis possible. 'Tis possible. But it sounds a bit too worthy. For me . . . 'tis freedom from starvin' I'll be lookin' for. An' I'll wager ye be out t' grab the round old pound like the rest o' us, or ye wouldn't be takin' these chances."

Mrs. Billington looked up from her cooking. "Well, 'tis plain why *we're* goin'. We want t' be rollin' in riches and blimey. I'll be havin' a red carriage with four jet black horses . . . an' rubies an' emeralds . . . an' live in a castle."

Mullins had to smile. She was artless and so credulous, poor woman, yet there was something about the courage of this buxom, ignorant *Hausfrau* that made him admire her a little. "I hope ye get what ye want," he said.

Governor Carver, however, looked at her sternly. "Madam, freedom alone warrants our daring in this pilgrimage. Most of us have sold our land and our possessions and have given all our money to make this voyage possible."

" 'Tis hard to believe in these modern times." Langemore shook his head and walked away.

"I wish we didn't have to have these strangers aboard," Edward Winslow remarked. "They don't seem very God-fearing to me."

"Edward, before we arrive these strangers, as ye call them, may all join us in our thinking." Brewster smiled and put his arm around the younger man.

"I must go and see to the rest of my family," Mullins said.

"And I must start preparing supper," Priscilla added.

"Ye don't need to fix anything for the landlubbers below," Mullins laughed as he stepped toward the companionway.

While they had been talking, the waves had become higher, and some passengers were clinging to the rails. The sailors scoffed with much hilarity and pointed and swore at these sufferers with crude remarks.

Priscilla's turn on the fire box came much later than expected. The *Mayflower* had begun to buck and roll like a young foal as she hauled porridge and water for her mother and Joseph, vegetables and meat for stew, and two large iron pots from below. She managed to get one of the pots on the tripod as the deck pitched. She stepped back for a minute and watched the other women struggling with similar problems with their own cooking. Suddenly the ship gave a lurch. Priscilla's pot swung off the hook and rolled across the deck toward some children, playing. She darted after it and, without thinking, picked it up. Immediately the hot iron seared into her hands, and she dropped it quickly. There was an immediate silence around her as people nearby looked at her red, swelling hands. Then she was aware of Mary Brewster, rushing toward her, and a crowd gathering around.

"Somebody get Doctor Fuller," Mary called out.

Then Clarke, the first mate, broke through the onlookers. "Stand back," he ordered. He turned to one of the sailors. "Get John Alden." The man ran to do his bidding.

"It's all right," Priscilla protested, holding her hands close to her. "Just let me have some cold water. I'm all right."

"Ye were foolish to grab that pot," Clarke said, and smiled, "but ye were brave."

Alden arrived, bringing a firkin of butter. Priscilla pulled her hand back as he reached for it, but he grabbed her wrist and, with his other hand, gently massaged the burn with the butter. A kind of sigh went up from the watching passengers as they saw Priscilla's hand relax, and presently, one by one, they drifted away.

Then the doctor arrived. "Sorry," he announced, "I couldn't leave Missus Tilley. She's very ill." He observed Alden, spreading the soothing remedy. "Ye're doing well, lad."

"He cares for us on the regular crew," Clarke stated with some pride.

"Can ye do the bandaging?" the doctor asked Alden.

"That I can," Alden replied, "if ye care to give me the permission."

The doctor studied Priscilla, who had not lifted her eyes. "Mistress Mullins, is it all right with thee?"

Priscilla looked at him, dazed. "It seems so," she replied, "but I had best sit down."

The first mate hurried to bring a barrel.

"Do ye feel faint?" the doctor inquired.

"A little," she answered.

Just then her father came running up. "They just told me," he said. Then he proceeded to talk with the doctor as Alden bandaged Priscilla's hands. When Alden had finished, Mullins took her arm and led her gently below.

Halfway toward the hatch, Priscilla turned. Alden was still watching her. "Thank thee very much," she said quietly.

Priscilla stayed with her family that night, although there was not much sleep with the throbbing pain. She stayed on with her family for the next day, but then returned to the captain's cabin for the night.

Constance Hopkins was brushing Priscilla's hair for her the morning after her return when there was a knock at the door. Constance went to open it. John Alden was standing there.

"Is Miss Priscilla here?" he asked. "How is she doing?"

"Come right in . . . she's getting along quite well."

Alden strode toward Priscilla. "How are thy burned hands?" he asked.

Priscilla did not miss the use of the intimate pronoun, but she knew full well that she, too, had used it.

"Oh, quite well, thank ye," she replied, looking up at him and held out her hands for him to see.

He removed the bandages while the other girls watched closely. He then took her hands into his own. She felt how large and strong they were, and how rough the skin was.

"Yes, they seem to be mending," he said. "Are they still very tender?"

She pulled her hands away gently. "Yes, I have to be careful."

"We help her," Desire broke in. "The poor thing cannot even lace her dress in the morning."

Priscilla turned her face down with embarrassment. "My hands shall be strong soon."

Alden replaced the bandages but cut off the parts over her wrists. "There . . . that will do for now. It will give thee a little more flexibility. The bandages may come off in a few more days."

"Thank thee muchly. I am very grateful," Priscilla replied, looking up at him again.

"If the . . . ," he started, looking at Priscilla, "if . . . any . . . of ye should need anything," he went on, facing the group, "just ask." Then he turned and was gone.

The girls went back to their work—all but Desire, whom Priscilla noticed was still looking after Alden.

Chapter Seven

As time wore on, excitement seemed to grow with the steady breeze and warm weather. The waters rushed swiftly past, giving a sensation of great speed. Perhaps, it was hoped, they would make landfall sooner than expected. They were already nearly halfway to their destination.

Governor Carver had decided it was time to start training a guard detail for the voyagers when they should land, for he had been warned of the hostility of the Indians. Captain Miles Standish, a man not of their faith but a soldier of fine repute, had been chosen in Holland to lead this group. William Mullins was to be one of them.

One gray afternoon, a few days later, Mary Chilton and Priscilla were finishing picking up after the singing class when Governor Carver, Miles Standish, and several other passengers came on deck, followed by the recruits.

Standish, red-haired and red-bearded, in coat of mail, helmet, and full armor stood commandingly, feet apart, arms akimbo. He watched as the recruits, also in armor, came toward him. Richard Warren, Edward Winslow, Isaac Allerton, Stephen Hopkins, and Priscilla's father walked over to Standish. William White then appeared, striving to fasten a coat of mail. John Crackston, William Butten, and John Howland trudged awkwardly across the deck. Priscilla was surprised to see that William Butten and John Howland, both gentle-faced youths of her own age, had been recruited, for they did not seem to be soldier material. And John Billington, that wretch.

Priscilla watched, surprised, as Alden strode up to them, obviously to join. "The captain wants the crew protected while we unload the ship and sent me as a volunteer," he explained.

"That's agreeable," Standish said tersely. He turned abruptly. "Fall in there! Atten-shun!" he ordered.

The men struggled into line, clumsily handling the disassembled muskets. Billington sat down on a keg.

"Not now, Cap'n," he said. "I've a mind t' rest. Too much retchin' with this rockin' ship."

Crackston agreed. " 'Tis the swayin' that gets me. Me an' my boy 'ave been sick all night. Will it ever stop?"

Shipley, standing with Jyp at the rail near Priscilla and Mary and a gathering group of passengers, broke in: "Sure 'twill, soldier. Just ye lean over the side there an' say . . . 'Be smooth, you, in the name o' the Lord' . . . an' the ol' sea'll just lie down like a tame dog." Shipley and Jyp doubled up, laughing, obviously enjoying the audience.

"That's blasphemy!" said young John Howland, one of the Separatists, turning toward the sailors. In an instant Shipley tripped him, and Howland, in his armor, clanked to the deck. Mullins and Winslow started to help him, but he rose as fast as possible and, red in the face, started toward Shipley. Collecting himself with great effort he said—"Either your feet are too big, my friend, or my walk is too slow."—and turned back to join the rest of the recruits. Shipley raised his fist behind Howland's back, muttering.

"Order, men . . . order!" Standish shouted. "Atten-shun! Do ye hear me? We *must* be prepared to protect ourselves from hostile Indians and any and all enemies." He gave Shipley a look. "Fall in! You, too, Billington."

The men arranged themselves in a sloppy line. With a sincere attempt at military procedure, they shifted places several times to make adjustments according to their height. Priscilla was pleased to see her father and, also, John Alden, standing stiff and straight.

"What *is* the matter with ye?" Standish fumed at the men. "Don't ye know the first order of military bearing?"

The men straightened up.

"That's better. Eyes front. Forward, march. Hup, two, three, four. . . ."

The men started off, bumping each other, some on the left foot, some on the right. Coppin came around the bulkhead and stood next to the sailors.

"Who is that cock o' the walk little shrimp over there?" Priscilla heard Shipley ask.

"Quit your jestin', Tom. That's Cap'n Standish. 'E's tryin' 'is best." He eyed Shipley curiously. "Ye're red o' the face. Be ye ailin'?"

"Naw, an' don't ye be starin' at me." Shipley turned away and shouted at Standish: " 'Ey, Cap'n Shrimp, 'avin' yer little troubles, are ye?"

"Ignore him, men," Standish admonished. "When I say hup, two, three, four, ye start marching with your *left* foot . . . your left foot first." The men stumbled back into a semblance of a line. "Now," Standish continued, "present arms!"

The men hesitated and then, except for Warren, Winslow, Alder, and Mullins, presented disassembled muskets.

"What is this?" Standish shouted, his face as red as his beard. "Assembled muskets only!"

"Sir," John Howland timidly ventured, "we don't know *how* to assemble them."

Standish stood with his mouth open. Shipley and Jyp started to laugh.

"Not know how to assemble a musket!" Standish demanded. "What kind of men are ye?"

69

"Peaceful men, sir, if so be, but fain ready to protect our settlement against attack, if need should come," Howland replied.

"We be not fightin' men," Bill Butten backed him up.

There was a general nodding and mumbling among the recruits, and among many of the onlookers. Standish spluttered in disgust. Shipley and Jyp held their sides, convulsed.

" 'Ey, Cap'n," Shipley gasped, "there be a couple a fine lads below knows all about muskets." He turned and, cupping his hands over his mouth, called out: " 'Ey, kids, ye're needed topside!"

Standish pretended not to notice. "Watch *me*, men. Set your rest here . . . that's this tripod. . . ."

The men tried to follow his example, the tripods slipping this way and that. Shipley gurgled and choked as Standish continued.

"Catch that lock, ye numskulls . . . that's it . . . now remove the *match* with your *left* hand. . . ." He watched, doubting. "Do ye know left from right? Ho! Good! *Now,* hold it between the fingers . . . with the thumb and forefinger. No! No! No, the *same* hand! Watch me! Hold the barrel *up* . . . like this. Now for the powder . . . now for the ball and wad . . . push it all in with the rammer . . . that's right!" He sighed. "Now . . . ready . . . aim carefully. Ye don't want to hit the ship. All right . . . *fire!*"

There was an explosion from several of the muskets; the rest misfired. Shipley and Jyp roared and whooped.

"Boom! Boom! *Bang!* That'll scare them Injuns. It sure scares me!" Shipley wiped his eyes and gave Standish a sweeping bow. "There be our stalwart army . . . God help us!"

The sound of the guns brought more people up on deck. Standish decided to forego the firing lesson for the day. "That'll do for the muskets, men. Stack them over there and

70

disassemble them later. We'll spend a bit o' time puttin' some heft on ye. Atten-shun! Fall in! Forward march! Hup, two, three, four. . . ." The men stepped off in unison this time. Priscilla suspected it was partly because of the audience. Finally, as the women came on deck to fix supper, he dismissed them. Mullins came over to Priscilla and Mary Chilton and sat down to rest.

In the distance the gray blanket of the sky had been subtly changing to a darker color. The water was nearly black, white caps silhouetted against it. Thunder rumbled off to the east. Suddenly an aureate arc lighted the sky, followed by a bellow of thunder directly overhead. Women and children, Mary among them, scurried back below. The men looked nervously upward. As the wind and waves continued to increase and the sky to blacken, the *Mayflower* began to pitch and roll.

Clarke called out from above: "Clear the deck! All passengers below!"

Mullins grabbed Priscilla's arm. "Let's stay in the lee of this bulwark and watch." They hurriedly slipped into the sheltered space.

The recruits hurried toward the hatch, but, as the ship rose on the crest of a wave and jarred into a trough, Howland, one of the last, grasped at a windlass. Mullins stepped out to help him, but Howland clung on tightly. Then Mullins saw Shipley coming across the deck. Shipley pried Howland's fingers loose and booted him down the steps. Mullins started to protest, but both he and Shipley were thrown against a bulwark.

Shipley reeled a bit and spat. "Ye lousy landlubbers!" he shouted above the storm and shook his fist in the direction Howland had disappeared. "I'll see to it personal . . . that 'un don't make port, or ye either." He glowered at Mullins, then he turned on Coppin. "Ye're the pilot! We shoulda took Columbus's route . . . south!"

"Too many pirates that way," Coppin answered, rolling with the ship. "Make fast those barrels, Shipley!" he then ordered.

Shipley staggered a few feet, hit the rail, and bounced back. "Pirates! Rather take me chances with them bloody pirates 'n face up t' what's comin'! I can smell it! Me for a slug o' rum!" He took a leather flagon out of his pocket and drank it empty. "Don't feel good," he mumbled to Coppin.

"Leave the rum be!" Coppin ordered as another flash of lightning brightened the deck. "And you, Mullins . . . get below!"

Priscilla shivered and slipped farther back into the corner, clinging to a lantern hook as best she could.

Another blast of thunder shattered the air over the ship. Mullins retreated but only back behind the bulwark with Priscilla. They leaned forward enough to see Clarke rush out on the poop deck followed by Captain Jones.

"All hands! All hands!" the captain shouted through the bullhorn. "Furl them sails!"

Sailors scrambled onto the deck and spidered into the rigging, grappling with the lines and struggling to lash the sails in the heavy blow. Quickly and expertly they worked. Sails slapped like musket shots as they were lowered. Priscilla and her father were thrown from side to side in the narrow space.

The *Mayflower* climbed tower-high on a wave, plunged into the trough, and in a crosswave turned abeam. A great wall of water broke over her. The vessel shuddered and twisted, first heeling to starboard, then to port. Mullins was thrown to the deck, but with Priscilla's help managed to struggle to his feet.

A fearful crack sounded on the main deck. Then Priscilla and Mullins heard screams from below decks over the storm.

"Help! Help! Get back below!" Clarke shouted, pointing a

finger at Mullins and Priscilla. The two, clinging together and sliding as the deck pitched, slowly struggled toward the companionway.

"Avast you, Alden!" Priscilla heard Clarke call out. "Get below! See to that beam!"

There was chaos in the damp darkness of the main cabin. Faces, shocked with terror, flared in the swaying lantern light. Water streamed from above with every roll of the ship. The hull cracked and snapped. Barrels, valises, pans, bedding, trunks, and furniture plunged about. Children and women, even men, screamed in panic as they tried to maintain balance.

There were anguished cries.

"The ship is sinking!"

"We'll all drown!"

Mrs. Billington's wails rose wildly above the rest.

Mullins and Priscilla found Alice and Joseph frightened but safe. As Alden followed them, they shoved their way through the wet bodies.

"Standish, bring a plank . . . and ye, there," he pointed at Mullins, "bring that lantern!" Alden looked up, studying the large crack in the deck's beam, water pouring in on him.

"The ship's breakin' up!" Billington shouted at him.

"Just enough water for a good fresh cool bath," Alden replied, not looking down.

"What's all the trouble, matey?" Coppin called, sliding down the hatch stairs as the ship lurched.

"It's a bad crack, Mister Coppin. This beam might break if we can't brace it."

"Oh my God! Save us! Get the captain!" Christopher Martin yelled, breaking through the crowd.

Coppin turned on him. " 'E's a mite busy above," he sneered.

Bedlam broke loose again among the passengers. Mrs. Billington's screaming and the children's wails pierced the dark. "We're all lost! It's damnation on all of us! My babies! My babies!" Mrs. Billington howled. She threw up her hands frantically, then grasped her boys to her bosom. The other children then cried loudly.

Alden looked down, annoyed. "Miss," he suddenly said, looking at Priscilla. "Take charge of those children."

Startled, Priscilla took Mrs. Billington's arm and shook her. "Quiet," she said firmly. "Quiet, all of you. Give the men a chance to fix this." She looked around. "Fetch that other lantern!" she said to Joseph, "and give it to Papa." Mullins was by this time aiding Coppin in firming the ladder for Alden on the slippery, wet floor.

Brewster stepped through the group from the dark. "Stand back and give the men room," he urged. "Do not be afraid. God will calm the storm as He did the sea before. He will not desert us."

" 'Tis sure we could use some outside 'elp t' get us through *this* tempest," Coppin remarked dryly.

Alden shoved a plank under the beam as the crack started to widen. The strain forced the plank to bow slightly.

"This won't be enough to hold it," Alden said. "Get the iron screw on the printing press. The deck's low, and it might reach."

Standish and Mullins took the lantern and disappeared into the darkness. The ship continued to roll and creak in the gale, and the passengers, in their terror, stood back and tried to brace themselves.

In a moment the men returned and, with Bradford's help, slowly pushed the heavy machine forward. Some of the wailing ceased as everyone watched the strange operation.

When the screw was directly below the crack, Alden and

Coppin began turning the bar on the side. Slowly the large black column rose until it touched the split beam. Then, as it was forced upward, miraculously the crack closed. A great cheer went up, and even Coppin joined in the short prayer of thanks Brewster offered.

"Ye are as good as thy reputation," Priscilla's father said, clapping Alden on the shoulder.

Suddenly they all noticed Howland as he ran up the companionway.

"Come back!" Coppin shouted, as he and Alden and Mullins hurried after Howland who disappeared above decks.

After rushing past Squint and Shipley on deck, Howland made straight for the rail and was sick.

Squint called after him: "Get back, you fool! You ain't allowed on deck!"

Coppin and Alden made their way slowly along the side of the ship in the driving wind toward Howland. Squint was of no help. He was struggling to support Shipley who was writhing and holding his stomach.

Jyp, swaying back and forth, was also trying to help Shipley and keep his own balance, and he cried out: "Tom, ye're drunk. C'mon, get below."

" 'M not drunk," Shipley moaned. " 'M sick, I tell ye . . . sick."

"Then watch out!" Jyp shouted.

They looked up to see an enormous wave as high as the mast, towering over them. The *Mayflower* rose part way on it, but it struck with tremendous force, washing over the deck with water three feet high. If Mullins hadn't been thrown against a cannon, he would have been washed overboard. When the wave passed, they all looked around for each other. Howland was missing.

"My God! He's swept overboard!" Jyp cried.

"Told ye he'd not make port," Shipley managed to answer with a hideous grin.

"Man overboard! Man overboard!" Coppin and Jyp both shouted as they ran through the water to the rail.

In the black, churning waters, Howland was nowhere to be seen.

"Throw out a line! Grab that 'alyard!" Coppin yelled.

"Fool. No use in this sea. 'E's lost," Shipley declared as he fell to the deck.

They all leaned over the side as Jyp threw out the rope. Alden had procured a lantern and waved it back and forth as he reached forward.

"Look! Look! I think I see something!" Squint shouted. "It's an arm . . . an arm wavin'! Looks . . . looks like 'e's caught the 'alyard!" He almost fell overboard, straining as another wave caught him. "Careful! We'll dash 'is brains out against the side o' the ship! *Pull! 'Eave!*"

Coppin tied the boat hook to another line and lowered it to the feebly moving man who was disappearing into a wave. The man rose again, and everyone watched tensely as Howland struggled to attach the hook to his clothes in the rolling waves.

"Get 'im up . . . don't swing 'im against the side!" Coppin shouted, waving his arms as if guiding the limp form dangling in the air.

Gradually Howland was dragged in by his belt over the side. He fell to the deck, unconscious. The sailors worked on him, turning him over and rolling his stomach on a barrel. One of Howland's hands slowly lifted, motioning the men to stop.

"He's alive!" one of the men cried out.

Then as Howland's heaving subsided, he opened his eyes and, after being helped to sit up, got on his knees.

"Thank Thee, Lord, for saving me," he murmured. He looked up, dazed, at all those around him. "I just grabbed . . . I just grabbed . . . anything. Ye say it was the halyard? Thank God!"

Then Shipley came staggering over to him. "Alive. More's the pity! Thank yer silly God. Yah! We're the ones as saved ye, not yer *God*." He reeled back, clutching his throat, and fell face down on the rail, retching.

"He's right," Howland agreed, "I owe ye my life. My thanks to God and to ye, too. I'll not be giving ye any more trouble." He bowed his head as the others helped him to his feet.

" 'Twas worth it t' see a man brought back from the fishes in such a gale," Jyp stated. "Nor in a million years could it be happenin' again!"

Coppin and Alden were helping Howland. Shipley was still slumped over the rail. He didn't move.

Squint took Shipley's arm, and the sailor slowly fell to the deck in a heap.

"Looks like he's passed out!" Squint called in the storm.

"Shipley drunk again?" Captain Jones demanded close down from above.

"Looks t' be more'n that, sir," Squint replied.

"Well, get Clarke . . . get the mate!"

Squint bent down, giving Shipley a shake as Jyp ran for Clarke. The men now all stood, braced against the rocking of the ship. Clarke came over and bent down to examine Shipley.

"He's gone!" the first mate declared.

" 'E can't be! 'E was talkin' t' us a minute ago," Squint wailed.

Then Coppin stepped forward and bent down, swaying with the ship in the calming storm. " 'E came topside a bit back sayin' 'e 'ad the fever. It's the sickness . . . the storm . . . an' 'is drink!"

Squint looked after Howland, shaking his head. "That one saved . . . an' this one dead. Your God is for certain on your side," he said with a strange look at the Separatists who were present.

Next day, on the waist deck, Shipley's body lay covered with a canvas on a plank, ready to be slid into the sea. The sailors were gathered at one side, huddled together, fear and superstition showing on their faces; Brewster and Howland and many of the Separatist group stood on the other side of the deck. Curious passengers hung about, half hidden behind the cannons and bulkheads.

The captain and two mates stood by the body while Alden and Jyp braced it. The wind and storm had passed on, leaving behind ash-gray skies.

Captain Jones spoke. "Ready, men!"

William Brewster stepped up to the captain. "Do ye mind if I say a few words?"

Jones looked surprised. "What for?"

"It isn't fitting to send a man to the next world without committing his soul to God."

"Many are those we've sent without a thought," the captain answered. "Besides, what's it to ye? This 'un gave ye naught but trouble. Like as not he'll go to hell, no matter what ye say."

"We bear the fellow no spite."

"Well, go ahead. It can do no harm. Keep it short." He handed Shipley's papers to Brewster. "Here's his name."

Brewster held up his hand. "Dear Lord, Thy servant, Thomas Shipley of Liverpool, has come to an untimely end. Judge him not, we pray Thee, by the sins he has committed but rather by the good he has done . . . for we know no man is entirely evil. In the name of the merciful Christ we pray. Now . . . to the waves I commit your body and to God I commit your soul. Amen."

Priscilla saw Shipley's body slide off the plank, and she shuddered. A long silence followed the splash. Brewster turned to his company and started them singing softly the new hymn he had learned when he went into hiding in Scotland. Brewster asked Dorothy Bradford, Priscilla, and Edward Winslow to lead the rest as he began in his low voice:

The Lord's my Shepherd, I'll not want;
He makes me down to lie.
In pastures green He leadeth me
The quiet waters by.
My soul He doth restore again,
And me to walk doth make
Within the paths of righteousness
E'en for His own Name's sake.
Yea, tho' I walk in death's dark vale
Yet will I fear none ill,
For Thou art with me, and Thy rod
And staff me comfort still.
My table Thou has furnished
In presence of my foes,
My head with oil Thou dost anoint
And my cup overflows.
Goodness and mercy all my life
Shall surely follow me
And in God's house forevermore
My dwelling place shall be.
Amen.

Once during the song, as Priscilla's eyes filled with tears, she looked up to meet Alden's glance. He made a wry face at her, and she quickly lowered her head.

As the song drew to a conclusion, the sailors returned to their duties, and the passengers drifted away. When Alden passed the Mullins family, he touched Priscilla's shoulder and whispered—"Ye sing nicely."—and then went on by. Priscilla noticed that it was the second time he'd touched her.

A few moments later Priscilla saw Dorothy Bradford go to the rail where Shipley's body had gone overboard. She stood for a while, watching the dull, flat sea. Presently her husband joined her. "What is it, my dear?" Priscilla heard him ask her.

She looked at him and back again at the water. "He is at peace now," she said.

Bradford took her hand. "Your sweet sympathy touches me. But, Dorothy, sometimes it pains me to see thee worry so much."

She slowly smiled. "And now it is thee who is worrying about me."

He put his arm about her as they left the deck and went below.

Chapter Eight

There were no more mighty gales, yet the discomfort aboard the ship caused much misery. Grateful as the voyagers were for the strong wind, the steady rain and increasing cold made being above decks a trial. All those going topside were drenched as streams of water knifed across the ship, blown by icy gusts.

Dr. Samuel Fuller, a Separatist who had come with the group from Holland, was called on night and day to attend to patients—Separatists, strangers, and crew. He was aided by his young assistant, William Butten, who never seemed too tired to care for a crying child or to run errands for the doctor. He was a handsome lad, and, when he himself became ill, the Separatists were eager to care for him.

Mrs. Carver, Mrs. White, and Mrs. Mullins all attended to his needs cheerfully. His young friends, too, brought him food, joshed him, and accused him of trying to get attention from the girls aboard. Richard Bitterridge, Peter Browne, and John Goodman, all of whom had come from Holland with him, accused him of playing ill to get the young women to read to him and bring him food. He took it all good-humoredly, even when it appeared he was much worse than expected. He continued, however, even in his high fever, to keep up his good spirits. When Alice Mullins, rising at four o'clock one morning, had found him gasping for breath in deep, agonizing spasms, the entire occupants of the cabin crowded toward him in prayerful silence. So it was that gentle young William Butten died.

At the services everyone who could find space on deck came to stand and listen. The Mullins family was crowded in at the back. Even the sailors were present for the doctor and his assistant had cared for their sicknesses, also. It was as if the loss of this young man had drawn them all together.

Elder Brewster spoke simply. "Many of us on this ship started out as strangers, one to another, but through adversity and sorrow we have become united. By God's grace alone we and this ship have been saved. William Butten was an exemplary person, giving his life in service to others. He served the Lord with gladness. We give thanks for having known him. God shall redeem his soul from the power of the grave, and he will live in the house of the Lord forever.

"God has been our refuge and our strength, a very present help in our time of trouble. Let us not, in our grief for this boy, lose sight of our purpose . . . God's purpose for us. We had come a long way before we arrived on this ship. Now we stand together as travelers, as pilgrims, as messengers of God, remembering how and why we came here, never forgetting to look forward to our freedom and to a certain glory, as William Butten did."

The pastor went on to bless the congregation and to give the last rites to the young man. A hymn was sung. Priscilla felt a strange sense of devotion, of dedication, of satisfaction, almost as if some stricture had been lifted from her spirit and she had been set free to follow with confidence wherever God led.

Life, like the ship, plunged inexorably forward. A few days later, at dawn, the sun burst over the waves, and the sight of it and the warmth of it brought a glowing feeling to all aboard the *Mayflower*. Sailors doffed their shirts, shocking the women, but the men were nonetheless proud to display their strong, muscular chests.

Clothes and bedding were hung from one end of the deck to the other in rows by special permission of the captain. Priscilla and the young ladies, Constance Hopkins, Mary Chilton, Desire, and Elizabeth Tilley gathered above on the deck of the sterncastle, ostensibly to do their tatting and lace work, but stealing glances from time to time at the recruits and other young men below them. Priscilla noticed Elizabeth Hopkins, watching John Howland as he trained with the guard group, and saw him look up at her and smile. Alden was not on deck, and Priscilla wondered if he had dropped out of the recruits or was just busy with some other task.

The captain, being in a good humor like everyone else, allowed the Separatists to have supper together above decks after this was requested by Governor Carver. So, for the first time since they had left Holland, they brought out their best clothes, lingered over their food, their hearts lifted once again with hope as they watched the beautiful sunset and enjoyed, as Bradford expressed it, "food and drink and friendly entertainment and Christian discourse and other real expressions of true Christian love."

Some of the strangers, the captain, the first mate, Clarke, and John Alden joined them. Too soon the cooking fires faded down to red embers, and the women began cleaning up. There was an air of peace, and people spoke quietly as they went about their chores. Mrs. Mullins stood up, stretching her back, and whispered to Priscilla who was wiping out pots and pans: "There is a soft breeze blowing tonight." She lifted her head, breathing deeply.

Priscilla looked up. "And it's warm, too, for October. Can it be the twelfth? I believe it is."

"It could be for ought I know. I've lost count of time."

Elder Brewster stepped into the middle of the group. "Come, all of you. Let us have evening prayer and songs to the Lord this pleasant night. Gather 'round and hold hands in a circle."

There were smiles and laughter as they took their places in the small confines of the deck. Priscilla was about to take Mrs. Tilley's hand when Alden stepped in between them. She was glad the dim lantern light hid her face as she felt his large, hard hand take hers. She dared not look at him but bowed her head as Elder Brewster began the prayer.

"This lovely evening . . . let us be grateful to Thee for bringing us nearly halfway to our destination. Through discomfort and illness Thou hast brought us closer together. For this we especially thank Thee. In Christ's name. Amen."

Once during the prayer Priscilla had stolen a glance at Alden, thinking this time to find his eyes closed. To her surprise, his head was not bowed, and he was watching her intently. Catching her look, he smiled broadly, and she quickly shut her eyes again. As they stood there, she started to let go his hand, but he held on tightly, pretending not to notice. Instead, he pressed her fingers as they listened to the prayer. Then Elder Brewster called upon Priscilla to start the singing.

Closer than heartbeat,
Closer than breath,
Touching our hands
In a pledge of our love.

Dear Lord, our Lord,
We want to be
Closer together.
Not to let anger,
Not to let greed,
Mar the luster of living,
The luster of love.

Dear Lord, our Lord,
Let us try being
Closer together.
Let nations desist
In their terrible might
From destroying the world
In one last tortured blight.

Dear Lord, our Lord,
May all people on earth grow
Closer Together.
This is our destiny,
This is our dream,
To show the way to
A New World of love.

Dear Lord, our Lord,
Let heaven bring us
Closer together.
Amen.

As the song ended, the voyagers returned to their fires and began picking up their things. Priscilla turned to Alden.

"We are glad you joined us, Mister Alden."

He turned his merry glance upon her. "I've been looking for a chance to do so for a long time." She started to join her family as they left, but he held onto her hand and pulled her back. "Let's stay here on deck a minute."

Priscilla looked at her mother, who smiled and waved as she disappeared below decks. "All right, for a minute," Priscilla agreed.

Nearly all the passengers had gone. Alden drew her over to the forward rail, behind one of the cannons. "A little more privacy here," he commented.

They stood watching the bow of the ship breaking the water into an ever-spreading white wing. The sky was black velvet studded with diamonds.

After a moment Alden spoke. "We're halfway across the ocean, and there's not been a chance to talk to ye."

"And whose fault be that?" Priscilla said airily.

"There's no bit of a chance to catch ye alone. Ye be so busy with this and that. Ye be always with your mother, or the children, or the other girls . . . or your brother," he dramatized the situation, making Priscilla laugh.

"Brothers may be sent off . . . if one has reason to do so," she teased, looking down into the water.

"Well, do not complain should the lad be missing next time we meet."

"And what do you intend doing?"

"Why, flip him overboard, what else?"

Priscilla looked back at him with an amused smile, but he kept a threatening frown. Then they grew quiet for a time, looking out at the silver-sprinkled sea.

"Ye were not with the recruits today," she commented.

"No. There is a longboat in the hold I'm building for ye, for fishing and exploring when we reach land . . . now that ye've lost the *Speedwell*. I'm building it in four parts and will put it together on shore."

"That will be a great help." Priscilla looked at him admiringly. "It will be much needed." There was a pause, then she asked curiously: "What decided ye to come on this voyage, Mister Alden? I know ye are not of our faith. Ye do not seem to be a very religious man."

Alden winced. "Yes. That's true, though it used to be different." He turned away from her, looking at the sky. "My father was the notable arrow-maker, George Alden. We lived with my mother and sister in All Saint's Parish in Southampton. He taught me to be a cooper and a cabinet maker and a joiner like him. He was a carpenter, that one." Alden looked down, leaning on the rail and stepping back. "They all died of the great plague . . . one after the other I had to see them go. As for religion, I lost my faith with them, I guess. I have their Bibles aboard . . . my mother's fine one . . . but I don't read them."

"I'm sorry. I had no wish to pry," Priscilla whispered.

"I just wanted to get away after they were gone . . . anywhere . . . anywhere away from England. So I went to sea."

"When was that?"

"A few years ago."

"Then this is not your first voyage on the *Mayflower*?"

"No, my third. She carried wine before, from France to the British ports. Ye and your company can be grateful for that. She's a sweet ship . . . from the wine . . . else she'd be right smelly and moldy in this weather . . . worse than it is, I mean." He grinned.

"It can't be possible." Priscilla shook her head. She paused before she asked: "Then ye'll be returning with her?"

"Probably. My mind is not made up yet." He looked at her closely. "Yours is a favorable company. I have come to respect and admire them and even"—he came closer to Priscilla—"to like them."

She looked up at him. "We have all grown closer on this voyage. How could we help it in such close quarters?" She threw up her hands in a helpless gesture.

Alden did not smile. He caught her hands in his. "So we have. And I hope we grow closer, too . . . thee and me."

Priscilla turned away slightly. She waited a moment before she spoke. "How many stars there are tonight! What is it the psalm says? . . . 'when I behold the stars in the sky, what is man that Thou art mindful of him?' " She turned back to Alden. "Ye must have felt that way when ye lost your family." She thought a minute. "Yet each star follows its own orbit . . . and with God's direction does not deviate. So it is for us."

"And a falling star?"

"That, too, is in God's plan. It must be, since the earth, the seasons, and we ourselves are miracles of growing and changing. We are truly complex wonders of perfect mathematical precision that could not possibly happen by accident . . . the objects of God's planning . . . of His own creation."

"Ye are well-versed . . . *and* ye are trying to reclaim me."

She smiled. "So I am, and as a Christian. And now . . . I must go below."

He put his arm across the bulkhead to block her way. "No, not yet. There be so many folk aboard this ship. I may not see thee alone again."

He put his hands on her shoulders and kissed her lightly, then drew her quickly to him. She felt the cold leather of his jerkin against her warm breast and the coarse rough wool of his breeches through the silk of her skirt. The solid strength of his arms and shoulders enfolded her. She felt protected, safe. Yet at the same time she felt herself pulling back a little. Putting a trembling hand gently over his mouth as he bent to kiss her again, she struggled to keep her voice steady.

"There's an old story about a tortoise and a hare, Mister Alden. Personally I've always admired the tortoise."

"Ah, but that was a chance occurrence." He tried to pull her to him again, but she drew away.

"And do ye consider this to be a chance occurrence?" She gave him an amused glance. He opened his mouth to speak, but she shook her head and went on. "And even if ye *do,* I would hope there might be other . . . ah . . . races? And that thee might think a little more deeply."

She turned quickly and walked away. When she reached the companionway, she spun around, stood looking at him a minute, and waved. He raised his hand toward her.

Then she hurried below decks.

Chapter Nine

Alden had been right. There was no time to be alone. Stormy weather and a sharp, biting wind plagued them. The sickness and the frigid, perpetual dampness continued to penetrate into the ship, causing colds, coughing, and more serious illness. Her mother called upon Priscilla to help cook and care for the family as well as to assist with the patients. Sometimes, as she and Alden passed, their eyes met and twice he had managed to say a few words closely and press her hand.

A restlessness began to grow among the passengers and crew. Blown far off course as the captain had determined, still they felt they must be somewhere near their destination. They had been at sea for almost forty days. There began to be dissension. Many of the men felt the vessel was no longer seaworthy, considering the crack in the main beam, although as yet it had shown no further signs of weakening. Still, her decks and upperworks were leaking, and at night she moaned and sighed with every wave.

In the main cabin there was a constant odor of mildew and rot. The women, especially, were annoyed. There seemed to be no way to get the linens, blankets, and clothes dry. On a dreary morning some of them gathered in the passageway. Priscilla and Alice were trying to mend some clothes but could not help overhearing.

"Me shoes be moldin' on me feet" Mrs. Billington was complaining. "An' me son John is down with the misery."

"We ought to be allowed some extra time on deck to dry our things," Mrs. White added. "And we've had very little hot food with the wind and the rain."

"As for sleepin', there's none," Mrs. Billington went on. "I 'ave not 'ad this 'ere dress off in days . . . an' the lice be *terrible!*" She scratched her bountiful waist and upper thigh.

Mrs. Hopkins, who was expecting a baby, sat down on a keg beside the older women. "And there's no fruit, nor even oranges, and no greens for weeks now."

"It's more than I can bear to stay below with the rats!" Rose Standish wrapped her skirts around her tightly. "There must be *hundreds* of them."

"Chisels it takes to eat the weevily biscuits, and ye rakes more crawling maggots off the top of the soup than there is vittles left," Mrs. White commented.

"At least, it's sometimes hot," Mrs. Carver said wryly.

Some of the men joined the group, it being their time to remain below decks.

"Pity there's not heat nor air below to dry out the mold on the insides of this cabin," Christopher Martin grumbled.

Brewster suddenly broke into the group. "This is enough of complaining. We must be willing to sacrifice to reach our goal. We should be thanking God for bringing us this far in safety."

John Billington turned on him. "*This* far? Who knows 'ow far we really be?"

"Or how far we were driven off course in the gale?" Martin elbowed the women out of the way to face Brewster.

Billington backed him up. " 'Tis said the ship's beginnin' t' fill with water in the 'old."

"We should come about now and go back." Martin spoke with some authority as treasurer.

" 'E's right," Billington said.

Alice Mullins did not intervene. Let the ship's crew make the decision . . . they know best. But she watched as, a few steps away, Dorothy Bradford turned around, her face brightening. She was listening intently.

"We're more than halfway now. It's just as dangerous to go back as to go on." Brewster protested.

"Some o' the tars theirselves as wants t' go back." Billington stuck his face forward at Brewster.

"I demand an assembly with the ship's officers and crew!" Martin exclaimed.

Accordingly, that afternoon there was a meeting on the deck. The captain was pressed hard to return to England by Martin and his supporters. The sailors were at variance among themselves, some wanting the money for the full voyage, some more afraid for their lives. Most of the Pilgrims fervently desired to press on.

John Alden was asked for his judgment as ship's carpenter. He concluded that, granted there were no actual tempests, the ship should be able to make land.

But in examining of all opinions, Bradford later recorded in his journal, *the master and others affirmed they knew the ship to be strong and firm under water, and for the buckling of the main beam, there was the iron screw, and the carpenter and master affirmed that the post under it would make it sufficient. And as for the decks and upper works, they would caulk them as well as they could, and though with the working of the ship they would not long keep staunch, yet there would otherwise be no grave danger, if they did not overpress her with sails. So we committed ourselves to the will of God and resolved to proceed.*

"If we keep her under sparse sail," Captain Jones told Governor Carver, "I'll wager a safe landfall."

Christopher Martin showed his disgust, and Dorothy

Bradford walked sadly away.

Day after dreary day the voyagers struggled with the problems of living. In the morning water had to be wrung out of their stockings. Clothes, hung on lines over their pallets the night before, were still damp. The small cooking fires on deck were insufficient to dry them out or warm the flesh beneath them. Many were ill with what Dr. Fuller diagnosed as typhus and scurvy.

Permission had been given in steady weather to keep the fires going most of the day, but supplies of wood and food, also, were getting low, and places around the fires were hard to come by. Sudden temper flare-ups were heard in spite of efforts on the part of nearly everyone to overlook the hardships.

Three things gave the passengers the incentive, if not to remain cheerful, at least patient. The first was the fact, recognized by the group thanks to Brewster's energetic guidance that misery causes persons either to pull together or to pull apart, and they did prefer the former. Bradford also enjoined them to remember the purpose of their journey and not to be daunted by the petty annoyances of daily living.

" 'Twill not be much longer now," Bradford encouraged them as he posted the chart that the captain was explaining. "True it is we have been blown far off course and with so many starless nights we cannot be certain how much farther we must go on, but landfall should come very soon."

Second was the exhilarating frolic of the twenty-four children aboard, fourteen and under, who were oblivious of the gray skies overhead. Hide-and-seek was their favorite game with the many places of concealment on deck. Occasionally the sailors would grumble, when stumbling over or into one or another of them, but even they enjoyed the unusual opportunity of watching the joyful diversions the children invented.

Third was the birth of a child to Elizabeth and Stephen Hopkins. The child was named Oceanus, and there was great rejoicing throughout the ship.

To offset the gloom of the weather, there was a feeling among the passengers of being one large, close-knit family. Yet there was one person abroad to whom neither the weather nor anything else seemed to matter. Alice Mullins and Priscilla observed that Dorothy Bradford seemed especially laconic. She acquiesced quietly to any suggestion, following the daily routine and doing her work as if mesmerized. Priscilla, being nearly the same age as Dorothy, sought a chance to talk with her alone.

One early foggy morning Priscilla, looking down from outside the captain's cabin, noticed a shadowy figure forward near the rail. It appeared to be Dorothy, and Priscilla took the opportunity of speaking with her. She approached slowly so she wouldn't startle the girl who was so very still and quiet.

"Good morning to thee, Mistress Bradford," she said softly, and, as the frail, lovely woman turned, Priscilla went on in a friendly voice. " 'Tis a good day to stay below with some quilting to do and a nice spot of tea, for it is surely a foggy day. Even the crow's nest is out of sight."

Dorothy looked up with a slight smile. "A good day for the children to play their game for they would hardly have to hide at all."

"Yes, and they would have no worry from the sailors, for it seems they are having tea, too. With no wind and the sails luffing, they have little work to do."

"No, there is none about. One of the children might fall overboard in this fog and not be missed."

"Possibly," Priscilla looked at her curiously, then she added more cheerfully, "but he would have to be an agile

94

climber for the side of the ship is rather high."

"Yes, of course, you are right." Dorothy smiled in a dispirited way.

"Do you remember when we visited Elder Brewster and his wife in Amsterdam? We attended your wedding, you know."

This time Dorothy looked at Priscilla with interest. "Yes, now I remember. We were both much younger then. Now here I am six years married with a five-year-old son." She paused. "You are as beautiful as ever, Priscilla."

"And so are you."

"Perhaps, but I am a great deal older inside."

Priscilla was taken aback by the sadness in the voice. "Come now. We are both a bit bedraggled by the unexpected length of the voyage, but we shall be fresh and happy again once we reach land."

"I hope so," Dorothy whispered.

"I know that you grieve for your little son, but no doubt he is well now, and, as soon as the winter is over, he will come across on the next vessel, for your husband has made arrangements."

Dorothy did not reply. She shook her head slightly.

"Did ye like Holland?" Priscilla asked, trying to change the subject.

At once Dorothy's demeanor brightened. "Oh, yes. I was loathe to leave. We had a very tiny house with many flowers around it in the summer and birds singing in their nests under the eaves of the thatched roofs. In the winter there was skating on the canals and muffins to toast in the big warm bonfires at the edge of the ice. We could skate for *miles* between the little farms on the bank, and there were many other skaters to stop and talk with. We and the Robinsons were close friends. He was our pastor, ye know, the one who married us.

We wanted so very much for him to come on the voyage with us, and he wanted to come, but, when many of our group elected to stay in Leyden, he felt it his duty to stay with them. They will help my mother care for our little boy."

"Do not fear, then. He is in good hands."

Dorothy looked down again, as if the conversation were at an end, but Priscilla tried one more advance. "We would like to have thee help us teach the children, or play with them, if ye choose."

Dorothy slowly shook her head as if considering it. "No, but thank thee."

"Let us talk again, then," Priscilla said as she started to leave, but Dorothy did not seem to hear.

Above, Captain Jones and Clarke came out on the poop deck. "There is that Mistress Bradford again," Priscilla overheard the captain remark.

"Shall I send her below, sir?"

"No, leave her alone. The poor woman seems much distressed." The captain sighed. "It is dank with mold below . . . so many ill we can't rightly stop them from coming topside. And they take risk and remedy *my* men, too. They do show their Christian love while we sailors let each other lie and die like dogs for fear of catching the misery."

Priscilla stepped back into a corner. She did not know whether she might startle them, so she remained where she was.

Clarke spoke. "It's like to turn to snow with the cold. Feels more like the midst of January than the Third of November."

They were quiet a moment looking ahead. The captain finally spoke. "We have been at sea fifty-eight long days. The landfall is much overlong in coming. What shelter these poor devils will have when we do make shore will take weeks or months to build with this weather and so many down with sickness."

"Some of the crew talk of naught else but putting them ashore regardless, and then heading the ship homeward. The rations are getting low," Clarke said.

"Well, I must protect my men first. These people will have to take their chances." The captain turned and, with Clarke, went back into the first mate's cabin.

A sudden sense of the danger of their condition caused Priscilla to put her hand to her throat with fear.

Mrs. Hopkins, carrying her baby and a basket of breechcloths, came through the hatch. She put the basket down and looked for a place to put the baby. Suddenly she noticed Dorothy Bradford.

"Mistress Bradford . . . I didn't see thee. Ye were so quiet."

Dorothy started. She seemed to take a long time to notice her surroundings. "Oh, I guess I was dreaming," she murmured.

"Well," Mrs. Hopkins said cheerfully, "would ye mind holding my baby for a moment? I need to stretch my line and forgot my hanging pins."

Again Priscilla started to step out with an offer to help but held back as Dorothy smiled and reached out eagerly. "He has a fancy name . . . Oceanus."

"A fancy name, indeed. It was my husband's idea . . . to remind us all of the voyage . . . as if we need reminding!" Elizabeth laughed.

"May God bless him with long and virtuous life," Dorothy added, looking down and caressing the baby's face.

"Amen. And your son, I am sorry he is not with thee."

"It was my decision," Dorothy said, not looking up. "I can never have another child, and I wanted him to be safe. I simply could not imagine bringing him on this voyage with the terrors we must face. And truly I am glad I did not." Then, recollecting the baby in her arms, she tried to soften her attitude. "You are courageous, and I am sure things will go well with you. I was caught in a vise. One way I might have lost my husband, had I stayed, and now I have lost my little boy."

"He is not lost . . . he will come across later," Elizabeth answered tenderly. She patted Dorothy's shoulder. "I must go below."

Dorothy studied the baby for a while, then she softly started to sing a lullaby.

Priscilla quietly stepped up the ladder and into the girls' cabin.

Chapter Ten

The afternoon of November 9th was dull and colorless. The heavy air and lagging wind had brought discouragement to all aboard the *Mayflower* the last few weeks. Inertia and weariness settled over the ship. Passengers straggled aimlessly about on the deck, and the sailors had not enough energy to curse, going about the necessary chores listlessly.

William Mullins and Joseph were sitting on barrels, the father whittling a seagull for his son. Alice and Priscilla walked slowly back and forth, trying to keep warm. Their hands were encased in muffs, and woolen scarves were wrapped tightly around their heads and throats. People standing around the fires were quiet and still, silhouettes against the leaden sky.

Mullins watched as Squint and Jyp stood at the rail, fishing. Squint shivered. "A dreadful cold winter already."

Jyp nodded. "And five of our men down with the fever."

"These fish do no bitin' just when we needs 'em so bad. Wait." He pointed down. "The water . . . look there. Looks like a different color."

"It appears to be . . . greener maybe?"

"Get the plumb line." He looked up at the crow's nest. "Endicott's supposed t' be up there, but I can't see him."

Mullins stopped carving as Squint returned with the plumb line and threw it over the side. He sniffed. "The air smells different."

Suddenly from up above came a cry. "Land ho! *Land ho!*"

Bedlam broke out. "I knew it. I knew it. I could smell it!"

Squint began dancing about wildly. Passengers rushed to the rails.

"Look, Joseph . . . *trees!*" Mullins called out.

"And a sandy beach," Joseph spoke, awed.

Alice grabbed Priscilla, and they embraced. "I don't know why I should have tears in my eyes," Alice said, laughing. Then they both ran to Mullins and Joseph. Mullins hugged his wife and did a little jig, Joseph trying to copy him.

"Birds, too," Alice added as two seagulls flew overhead.

The thrill of the moment caught all of them as they gazed at the land that was to be their home. From below people began streaming on deck, shouting with joy, and running from one vantage point near the rail to another. Some who were ill were helped or carried to observe the shore. Joseph was nearly crushed in the hysteria.

Cries of—"We're here!"—"Land! Land!"—"Thank God!"—were shouted all over the deck. Women were crying and laughing. Men clasped each other and slapped each other on the back.

Priscilla drew a deep breath and smiled happily as Alden joined them, putting his arm around Priscilla and his hand on Joseph's shoulder.

"It's a moment to fix in the mind," he stated.

Captain Jones called out from above. "Get back from the rail! Clarke! Coppin!"

The mates, standing on the poop deck, as transfixed as the rest, hurried down the ladder. Brewster and Carver assisted Clarke in moving the people back.

Then Brewster called for silence. "Come, everyone. Gather ye here in the center of the ship. Let us give thanks to Almighty God for safe deliverance." He bowed his head and knelt down. All the passengers who were able did the same and also most of the sailors, following the captain's example.

"Lord, Thou hast brought us by Thy mercy over the vast and furious ocean, and hast delivered us from all the perils and miseries of it for sixty-four days. And on this Thursday, the Ninth day of November in the year of our Lord Sixteen Twenty . . . a day we will never forget . . . our hearts overflow with gratitude to Thee. Amen."

Alice Mullins noticed that Dorothy Bradford still stood at the rail, looking toward the land. Mrs. Hopkins went to stand by her, holding her baby up, showing him the view. "See, little son, your future home."

Dorothy turned away, and Alice heard her say: "It appears to be a gray land . . . unfriendly and cold." She shivered and turned to go below.

Alice walked along with her. "We will make it warm. You will see, though it may take a little time. The sun will shine again."

"Whenever that may be," Dorothy replied coldly. "It appears to me we shall all die here." She went below. Suddenly it was Alice who shivered.

The excitement soon turned to speculation as to their actual location on the map. Brewster, Carver, Bradford, Mullins, Isaac Allerton, Edward Winslow, Christopher Martin, Richard Warren, Clarke, and John Alden gathered around hastily brought tables where Captain Jones had spread his charts.

Carver asked the question on everyone's mind. "Where do you make us out to be, sir?"

"Right here is where we are . . . off Cape Cod." The captain pointed to the spot.

Carver showed his disappointment. "Then we are far north of our intended landing place."

"We are not too many leagues from Hudson's River . . . but ye are wiser to settle here."

"And why would that be?" Bradford asked.

"There should be shoals to the south called Tucker's Terror, known to be hazardous even in fine weather. At this time of year they are fraught with peril."

Christopher Martin spoke up. "I am for staying here. We will be out of the territory of the merchant venturers and, therefore, free of our huge, miserable debt to them."

"Would we be free of England's jurisdiction?" Allerton asked.

"That we would," Martin loudly replied. "Our patent is for the Virginia Company, and this is the territory of the New England Company, not yet under English law. I am for staying here."

"But, gentlemen," Brewster held up his hand. "We must stand by the contract we have signed. The London merchants have paid for your passage and supplies, and we are bound to pay off that debt."

"We must be honorable." Carver spoke firmly but softly, trying not to anger Martin further.

Martin's face became red. "Ye are *fools* if ye do not seize this opportunity. Ye have heard what the captain said. It is certainly not by any fault of ours that as a result of being blown off course and through weeks of suffering we have been forced to land here."

"But Martin, ye were the one who signed the contract," Bradford reproached him.

"Only to get us out of Southampton," Martin equivocated. He looked at the cold, silent faces around him. "I intend to consult with the others, and ye may be assured they will agree with me." He turned abruptly and left.

Carver turned to the captain. "We must go south!"

Captain Jones shrugged his shoulders and went out on the deck. "Prepare to raise anchor!" he ordered. "All hands!"

The *Mayflower* then proceeded southward through seas becoming steadily more turbulent, as the captain had warned; and, as if the sky were in sympathy with the sea, the clouds darkened. Water began to swirl around the sides of the vessel in white-crested currents. Black waves crossed from all angles, and the ship shuddered and twisted.

"Enough of this!" the captain in the main cabin finally shouted to Carver. "I will not risk my ship or the lives of all those aboard. We are returning to the Cape. Ye may decide where ye wish to be landed later on." He went out on deck and roared out the command to turn back.

Inside the cabin, the men looked at each other with relief. They had not wished to ask the captain to change his orders again, but the terrible pitching of the ship had alarmed them mightily.

" 'Twould be a strange finale to our journey should the *Mayflower* founder here after so many long weeks," Bradford said wryly.

When the ship was out of danger and headed back toward the Cape, Brewster sighed and shook his head. "Now another decision must be made by the passengers. Fetch all of them to the deck."

When they were all gathered, including the captain, Brewster began. "We have seen that it is not safe to reach Hudson's River by this route. The captain says it will be necessary to put out to sea again for several days . . . perhaps a week in foul weather to reach our assigned destination."

Martin did not give him time to speak further. "I am for remaining where we first sighted land," he interrupted. "There is a fine bay where we will be somewhat sheltered from storms. It will also be a protection for the ships which come to take back to England our goods for barter. Surely on such a long, fine beach with hills behind it we will find a fresh-water river or stream. It looks a fine place to land."

Several men spoke up in agreement.

"And is that *all* ye wish, brother Martin?" Bradford asked.

Martin turned on him. "Ye know how I feel about the repayment of the debt."

There was a silence.

Brewster finally spoke. "There is more to be considered than debts and contracts and a convenient place to land. We who plan to make a community in this new country must not become renegades, with each person grasping greedily for himself. We all must, in a way, be servants to the communal debt, for the ship and for our passage. Due to the misfortunes of our embarkation it may be many long months, or even years, before this debt is paid, so there will be little difference between boundmen and freemen."

"I do not intend to be liable for more than the shares I purchased, and they are already paid in full," Martin protested. "It was an outrageous, unfair contract the merchants demanded, making slaves of us all, and they do not deserve to be paid off."

"I agree with you," Brewster declared, "but to save what we had already invested we had to meet their terms . . . and to obtain further necessary supplies from England we are *all* liable according to the contract."

Edward Thompson, William White's boundman, stepped forward. "Is it true that here we would not be forced to abide by *our* contracts and would *all* be free men?" he asked Carver.

"We will not force ye," Carver replied, "but we expect ye to be men of honor."

"To hell with honor!" Thompson shouted. "No choice had I but to be poor. Now, at least, I will be a free man, and no one can stop me."

There were shouts of—"Aye!"—"Aye!"

Thompson went on, glaring at Carver. "You forget that we boundmen and servants together with other passengers who wish to be free of debt come close to outnumbering you. And the crew, too. They, being anxious to return home, will be on our side."

"Are you, then, threatening mutiny?" Carver demanded.

"That we are!"

Then, to Mullins's surprise, Robert Carter, his own servant, stepped forward. "Let us not act hastily," he began. "In truth, we are not ill-treated in this group . . . and in that wilderness"—he pointed shoreward—"our masters must work as hard as we. Some of ye here are escaping debts at home and would be in jail in England. Here we can *all* begin afresh. Let us abide by our contracts. Let us work our way to freedom, and stand up as proud men."

There was murmuring among the boundmen, and Mullins could not tell whether it was aye or nay. He gave Carter a friendly pat on the arm as the man stepped back alongside him.

"Brethren all," Bradford said, "we must combine ourselves, or we will all perish." He rapped a belaying pin on the top of a barrel, and his voice rose. "Let us have order! Let us not fail when we have, at last . . . the chance to govern ourselves. We must have laws to guide us to our common goal . . . for the welfare and good of all."

"We will sound out the sentiments of each man on board," Brewster said. "In fairness and with justice for all . . . if we take the captain's advice and remain here on Cape Cod . . . let us draw up a compact and let each man have his say in its writing and his signature on it."

"It is a just way," Bradford said.

There were nods of agreement and then cries of—"Aye." —even from some of the boundmen.

★ ★ ★ ★ ★

It was Saturday, November 11th, when the *Mayflower* finally dropped her anchor in the shelter of the Cape. All night there had been an undercurrent of muffled but excited voices: arguments, whisperings, and gatherings of small groups forward in the main cabin near the Mullins family where the proclamation was being composed. Priscilla had chosen to remain with them for the night. The passengers had difficulty in sleeping for suddenly a voice would rise in protest and be hurriedly quieted. There would be silence for a minute, then the whispering would get louder, and the whole process would begin over again.

In the morning the voyagers, feeling this was to be an event, turned out in their best but warmest clothes. As they came on deck, a few spoke softly as they looked eagerly at the land, but everyone was solemn. The day was very cold, but sunny, with winds that blew across the deck in occasional gusts.

A table stood prominently at the forward end of the main deck. Most of the men assembled before it. Several of them wore their hats to emphasize the importance of the occasion. John Alden had been given Elder Brewster's hat that he waved with gusto as the Mullins family appeared. Brewster, Bradford, and Carver stood behind the table. Priscilla noticed that Martin had gathered a group of servants and boundmen around him.

The women and a few children grouped themselves at the rails and behind the men. At the back the girls—Priscilla, Constance Hopkins, Desire, Elizabeth Tilley, and Mary Chilton—were gathering. Peter Browne, John Goodman, and Richard Warren of the religious group and Edward Dotey, Edward Leister, and George Sowle, a handsome young boundman, stood beside them.

Brewster held up his hand for attention and waited for complete silence.

"Let us, as we undertake this momentous written compact of civil rights for us all, be mindful of the words of our beloved, wise pastor in Holland, John Robinson, who wrote us, and I read from his letter . . . 'The plans for your intended civil community will furnish continual occasion for offense, and it will be as fuel to the fire unless ye diligently quench it with brotherly forbearance and great love.' And he goes on to remind us, and I again quote . . . 'to yield to our elected officials due honor in their lawful administrations, not beholding in them the ordinariness of their persons, but God's ordinance for your good.'

"Let us, then, give respect and honor to our present governor, John Carver, and so be it . . . after the reading of the compact . . . that we approve it, and we will then elect our officials and every man shall have a vote."

Brewster then sat down, and Carver rose.

"I read for your approval the *Mayflower* Compact we have drawn up. 'In the name of God, Amen. We whose names are underwritten, the loyal subjects of our dread sovereign, Lord King James, by the grace of God, of Great Britain, France, and Ireland king, defender of the faith, *etcetera*. Having undertaken, for the glory of God and advancement of the Christian faith and honor of our king and country, a voyage to plant the first colony in the northern parts of Virginia, do by these presents solemnly and mutually in the presence of God, and one of another, covenant and combine ourselves together in a civil body politic, for our better ordering and preservation and furtherance of the ends aforesaid, and by virtue hereof to enact, constitute, and frame such just and equal laws, ordinances, acts, constitutions, and offices, from time, as shall be thought most meet and convenient for the general good of the colony . . . unto which we promise all due submission and obedience. In witness hereof we have hereunder subscribed our names at Cape Cod the Eleventh of November, in the year of the reign of our sovereign Lord King James of England. *Anno Domini* Sixteen Twenty.' "

Carver looked up. "Here I will affix my signature, and the rest of ye follow. I will call your names as ye sign." He handed the paper to Bradford, who also signed. Then Edward Winslow, Brewster, Allerton, and Miles Standish came forward to sign as they stood in line. When it came time for Martin, he flushed, looked about him in embarrassment as the expectant crowd watched him. Then abruptly he came forward and affixed his signature.

Next was Mullins, and, as he returned to his place, he smiled at his wife and Joseph and Priscilla.

After William White, John Alden was next in line.

"I am one of the ship's crew," he protested, but seeing the smiling faces around him and Priscilla's encouraging nod, he proudly walked forward and signed his name. When he had finished, he returned to stand with the young people's group.

"Does this mean ye are going to stay?" Priscilla whispered to him.

"It looks that way," Alden replied, winking at her.

Desire Minter, standing between Edward Dotey and Edward Leister, began murmuring and laughing with them but glancing at Alden as she did so. "Priscilla, ye are so fortunate to be so tall," she said, standing on her tiptoes. "I can't see a thing! Do ye think ye could find me a box to stand on?" She smiled appealingly at the two Edwards. They looked at each other, then suddenly swept her up. She let out a little shriek as they swung her on top of a bulkhead. Several of the women turned around, and one of them shushed her. Desire took no notice, looking down at Alden with a giggle and a toss of her head.

"Mister Warren . . . it's thy turn to sign," Constance Hopkins then said, nudging him.

He looked forward quickly for he, too, had been watching Desire. "Oh, of course." He strode toward the table to sign.

"Thee, too, Mister Browne," Constance reminded him, and Peter went on to join Warren. He was followed by John Howland.

Then George Sowle spoke up. "Sir," he addressed the governor. "May a boundman sign, too?"

"Of course," Carver answered, "that's the purpose of this paper . . . that we may all . . . pilgrims in a strange land as we are . . . be bound together as one family, with the precepts of God and Christ as our guide."

Then Sowle walked proudly forward amid the approving looks of the assemblage.

Thomas Tinker and Roger Wilder then wrote their names, and next in line was John Billington, who was given a push by his wife Ellen.

"Get ye up there," she said in a loud voice, "so everyone'll know ye're some'at important!"

Three more signed, then Edward Dotey and John Goodman, arm in arm, walked up to the desk, signing their names with a flourish and a bow to the entire group. Edward Leister hung back.

"Go on then, silly boy," Desire coaxed, but he only turned his face shyly against the wall. "Not in front of all these ones," he whispered.

Suddenly Edward Thompson called out from among the group who had been desirous of breaking their contracts. "I, too, will sign," he said in a loud voice, "for if so many of ye, with your great debts, feel it is just, then we must go on with ye. Ye are brave people, and we would be fools to go on our own in this wild and unknown place." There were sounds of acclamation from most of the crowd, but murmuring from among the dissenters, some seeming to approve and others to frown.

Thompson gestured toward the forest. "Who knows what hides there? It will be difficult enough for all of us, even if we stay together." He then signed his name.

"Forty-one of the forty-six men among us have signed," Carver announced. "Are there others?" He looked at John Langemore, Martin's servant, but the man slowly shook his head.

Mullins whispered to his wife. "Where is Carter?"

"He came down with a fever this morning," she replied. "Perhaps it has gotten worse. I must go to him when this is over."

"Mayhap he can sign later, then. He will be sorry to miss this."

The governor waited a few minutes. "Are there others?" he repeated. "Then the matter is closed." He took the paper and stood aside. "May the Lord bless our joining together in this *Mayflower* Compact and in all its future observance."

Brewster then stepped up. He announced that the election for governor would take place and all who signed the Compact could vote. When John Carver's name was mentioned, the election was unanimous in his favor.

Carver stepped back to the head of the table and thanked the group. "Now we may proceed with the main wish on everyone's mind. With Captain Standish's permission, we may go ashore."

Immediately there were loud cheers and much excitement. Standish shook his head, motioning for quiet. "Not at this time!" replied the little man dressed in full armor. "Not until the area has been fully scouted." He cleared his throat loudly. "There may be Indians." Cries of disappointment followed.

"But today is Sunday," John Howland called out, "and we keep the holy day and cannot go ashore then."

"I will take a contingent of men with me today," Standish went on. "William Bradford and thirteen others in full armor. We will make a survey and report to ye upon our return."

There was a breathlessness in the crowd. No one spoke or moved for a moment. After so many weeks, some were actually going ashore in this strange place. Then the men called upon, Mullins among them, hastened to obey orders and went below, followed by the straggling passengers. A few chose to remain above, although the wind was turning colder and snowflakes were flying across the deck.

Governor Carver approached Alden. "We are pleased and proud that ye are joining us," he said, shaking Alden's hand. "We shall soon be needing the shallop . . . the longboat . . . for exploration along the coast. The boat, as ye know, was separated into pieces for transportation. Will ye put it together for us?"

"Gladly, sir. I have already planned for this, but it will take some time."

"I'm aware of that," the governor replied, "but can ye give us an idea of how long it will take?"

"A week, perhaps two. We will have to caulk her as we go, and each caulking must be thoroughly dry before the next section can be added."

"I see," Carver replied. "Then, let us begin as soon as possible. We must scout a place near a river for our settlement very quickly, and it will be easier and safer for your help." He smiled and left the group of young people on deck to go below.

"How large is this shallop?" Priscilla asked.

"It can carry as many as thirty people," Alden explained. "I'll be going down to the hold to get it ready for work in the

111

morning." Alden turned to the men. "Come along if ye wish." Warren and Sowle joined him, and, as the three men left, Alden glanced over his shoulder at Priscilla with an intimate look.

Peter Browne walked over to the rail. "If only we could have been among those going ashore," he said fretfully. "I wish I could have gone."

"He took mostly the members of the guard," Priscilla said. "What do ye think they will find?" she asked, looking at the shore.

Browne snorted. "Snow and trees and Indians, no doubt."

"Friendly Indians . . . do ye think? My father is going," Priscilla said.

"Oh, it's too cold," Browne hastened to add, "even for Indians!"

Everyone laughed.

"Do they run about, as some say, with only a feather and some leather breeches and practically nothing else?" Desire giggled, blushing and putting a hand over her mouth.

"Maybe in the summer. You'll probably have a chance to see for yourself," Browne teased. "But 'tis the furs they'll wear in weather like this. That's what we'll aim to trade them for . . . furs."

"And we'll get a few of our own, too," Dotey added.

Browne gazed pensively back at the shore. "We need to find game to eat . . . and fresh water."

"Let's hope they remember that . . . while they're spying about for Indians," Dotey said.

Browne said: "Besides game and fresh water and timber for our houses, we need a river deep enough for large vessels and a flat place that can be easily defended for our settlement."

Priscilla looked at Browne. "That's a great deal to ask, and hard for the men in this damp and cold."

Just then her father came on deck, and she noticed how straight and handsome he was in his armor. She was proud of him.

Now everyone began coming topside again. No one wanted to miss the thrill of watching this first landing party. The men climbed into the *Mayflower*'s shore boat amidst a babble of excitement and encouragement. They waved to the crowd along the rail as the ropes began lowering the skiff.

As they began to pull away, there were cheers and shouts of good wishes. Almost everyone watched until the boat was beached and then began going back below.

Suddenly behind the younger group there was a commotion. Two dogs, a mastiff and a smaller one of mixed breed, bounded along beside Alden as he emerged from below decks.

"I let them out of their cages for some exercise," he laughed as the dogs began jumping around and barking.

"Poor things, they must be miserable down in the dark hold," Constance said, fondling the smaller dog.

"Here is something for them to chase," Warren added, tossing a large cork float across the deck. The dogs raced after it, the mastiff retrieving it and proudly bringing it back to Warren. On the second time the smaller dog reached the cork first but yielded it when the large one came at him. Then Warren threw the cork to Alden, who threw it to Edward Leister who threw it to Priscilla, the dogs leaping wildly, trying to follow it. Priscilla tossed it to Peter Browne, then it went to Desire, who dropped it as the dogs jumped on her. She went down with a cry, and everyone ran to her.

"Are ye hurt?" Alden said, kneeling down beside her.

"Oh, I don't know," she said hesitantly. She clutched at her wrist and rubbed her forehead. "I can't seem to catch my breath . . . I was so frightened." She looked around the group, then started to sit up. Alden helped her to her feet, and she swayed unsteadily. "Would ye help me back to my cabin, please?" she asked, leaning against Alden.

The game broke up then, Constance and Elizabeth going along with Desire and Alden. Priscilla, seeing Desire so well cared for, stayed on deck with Peter Browne and Richard Warren. She watched as Alden carried Desire up the ship's ladder. He was only performing an ordinary kindness, she told herself, yet it bothered her. And it did seem he remained a very long time in the cabin. She reprimanded herself for these ungracious thoughts and, excusing herself, went below to see her family and to see how Carter was faring.

Her mother was not in their cubicle, so she headed back toward the stern of the ship. As she had feared, her mother was there, bending over Carter. He was very red in the face; his eyes were closed.

"You had better get Doctor Fuller," her mother said, "and quickly."

The doctor was asleep in his hammock, and his wife was loathe to awaken him. "He's had so little sleep the last few days with so many ill."

But the doctor heard her. "What is it, Ann?" he asked sleepily.

" 'Tis Priscilla," she replied, and the good man rose fully dressed as he had taken to sleeping. Over his wife's protest the doctor yawned and followed Priscilla.

" 'Tis the pestilence again," he whispered to Alice, shaking his head. "Give him some brandy to strengthen him and some cool cloths to bring the fever down. Some of my elixir will help to make him more comfortable. We'll see tomorrow how he fares."

"I cannot leave him," Alice said, "so Priscilla, will ye get the elixir and some cool water, and, while ye are on deck, keep an eye on Joseph and watch for thy father."

It was getting dark when the news was called down to the main cabin that the shore boat was approaching. Priscilla had been up and down the companionway four or five times as the family was beginning to worry. Now excited cries were heard on deck.

"Ye go up and greet him, Priscilla. Take Joseph." Alice sat back on the stool with a sigh. "Carter seems to be rallying a bit, but I'd better stay with him."

Priscilla and Joseph heard calls and shouts as they went topside. The shore boat was being raised over the side, and the throng of people almost smothered the men as they climbed onto the ship. They were hailed and hugged in welcome. In the crowd of eighty or more people it was difficult for Priscilla and Joseph to reach their father.

"What was it like, Papa?" Priscilla tried to ask as she kissed him—but no one seemed to be able to hear anything in the tumult. Priscilla glanced around for Alden, but she could not see him in the thick crowd.

At last Standish stepped up on the ladder and addressed the gathering. He waited importantly for silence.

"Good news," he stated in his abrupt manner. "The land is fertile for farming. Trees aplenty for building."

Immediately a cheer went up.

"Attention!" Standish held up his hand again. "We came not on any Indians."

There was another cheer.

"That is not to say there is none about. Some bad news. We proceeded a short way along the beach. Ponds and marshes are all salt water. No streams or rivers. Further exploration for our location of settlement will be necessary."

There was silence.

Then, after a pause: "Permission is hereby given for all to go ashore on Monday."

A clamor of joy went up on the *Mayflower* that shook the masts, and shouts of—"Praise the Lord!"—were heard all over the ship.

There was laughter and even tears, and some of the passengers began dancing about, linking arms together and singing.

Chapter Eleven

On Monday, the *Mayflower*'s shore boat was rowed back and forth as the eager passengers hurried to reach land. The men had gone first to make sure the area was safe, and then boatload after boatload of women and children were landed on the beach. As more and more children arrived, bedlam broke forth. They ran and skipped and capered about like spring lambs. Nor did the snow and cold deter the women from gathering in groups to talk and laugh and enjoy the solid ground, the chance to inspect the area, and the freedom from confinement. Some had brought clothes and bedding and spread them on the bushes to dry. Many of the men went about feeling and studying trees as if they had never been seen before. Children gathered bunches of salt grass to play with. When they discovered a spring with fresh water, everyone scooped it up gleefully with their hands and drank.

Priscilla and Joseph and their mother stood with a large group. "The sand feels funny, like it's rocking," Joseph said, swaying back and forth.

"Yes . . . me, too," Wrassle Brewster giggled, almost falling as he reached over for a shell.

"I want to go play in the woods." Love Brewster tugged at his mother's arm.

"Stay here. There may be Indians about."

"Ha! And they'll get your scalp," Mrs. Billington teased.

"Mama, I'm afraid . . . what's a scalp?" Little Ellen Winslow looked around at the grown-ups.

"*Please,* Mistress Billington. Don't say such things in front of the children," Elizabeth Winslow protested.

Joseph stood up. "Who's afraid of Indians? I'm not." And he went running off with John Billington.

"See here," Alice Mullins called. "Ye are not to go near the woods."

But Joseph had run off down the beach and made no sign of having heard.

"If we contact the Indians, my husband is determined to make friends of them," Mrs. Brewster said, watching Love and Wrassle as they ran after the other boys.

"The men have finished gathering wood and are lighting a fire. Let's join them," Alice said. "This cold penetrates."

The group started up the bank.

Priscilla looked for Alden, but he was not to be seen, and she supposed he was back on the ship, working on the shallop. She surveyed the wild wastes of the beach and brush and woods ahead as she walked, sand filling her shoes. Would it really be possible for them all to live in this desolate land? Would there actually be houses and even farms here? Would she and perhaps John Alden . . . ? She quickly put the idea out of her head. The whole picture of a town in this forest was as impossible to imagine as . . . as Plymouth, England must have looked from Roman times.

As the women approached the big, blazing fire, Governor Carver was calling the men together. He motioned for Elder Brewster, Bradford, Standish, and Captain Jones to gather close. Then he unrolled a large, worn chart and laid it on a rock.

"This is where we stand now," he said, pointing to the paper, "but we must have more fresh water than this one small creek." He gestured to Coppin who was standing nearby. "Ye say ye have been in this region, Mister Coppin?"

"Come along this shore, we did," the mate answered, "with Cap'n Smith, and went t' beach in the longboat, but 'twere far south o' this 'ere place."

"We are in urgent need of a better location . . . and soon," Bradford spoke up. "We have to begin building. Would it be faster to scout by land or by the bay?" He turned to Standish. "And which way will be safer?"

"We should go up by the beach until the shallop is ready," Standish replied. "We cannot take enough men in the small boat to protect us in case of an Indian attack."

"Then we shall wait for the shallop, but we must proceed to scout by the beach as soon as possible."

He was interrupted by shouts from four or five of the boys, running out from the woods.

"Look! Look what we found!" Joseph came running up to his father, carrying a clay pot.

John and Francis Billington and the Brewster boys ran in after him, carrying more pots, feathers, and long brown stalks of a strange plant they were using for swords.

"And pointy houses, too . . . like funny hats!" Francis Billington said. "We peeked in."

"There's a place looks like a village . . . an Indian village," Joseph reported. "With beads and feathers. There's *bones*, too . . . all over." He cast a sidelong glance at John Billington. "We were going to keep it a secret, but maybe ye should come see." He stopped and looked at his father.

"Ye had no right to run off, Son, and ye know it." Mullins frowned.

"An Indian village!" Standish exclaimed. "Count the children. Come," he beckoned to the men, "we'll investigate. Be on guard."

"Don't worry. It's deserted," Joseph called softly after them.

"Son, I am displeased with thee."

"But look, Father, look what's inside the pot. Seeds."

Mullins poured the seeds onto a rock as a large group came around to look.

"So they are. Could they be . . . perhaps they are from the maize we have heard that the Indians eat."

There was a field of these stalks growing there, too," Joseph hurried to break in, trying to redeem himself.

"The boys are right," Standish asserted as the men rejoined the group. "It is an Indian village with a stand of maize growing alongside it. Strange it wasn't cut. We must be on guard. Arms always at the ready."

"Ye should not have taken anything" Brewster reprimanded his sons. "These do not belong to us."

"But we can plant the seeds," John Billington, Sr., broke in.

"Let us wait till we have met with these Indians," Brewster insisted. "We must return what we have taken."

Billington was about to protest when suddenly there was a scream.

"An Indian!" Mrs. Winslow cried out. "There. Right behind that tree."

Mullins instinctively grabbed Joseph close to him. "Where?"

"I saw him, too," Elizabeth Hopkins cried out, hugging her baby closer.

Standish and several of the men ran toward the tree. "After him, men! Bradford, Mullins, Allerton, Howland, and Warren . . . come with me! The rest of ye guard the women and children. Get them back on the ship. Remember. Arms always at the ready!"

"Wait, Miles. There must be *no* shooting," Brewster said. "If we were lucky enough to find these Indians, we will make peace. Keep that in mind."

Priscilla, Alice, and Joseph watched as the men marched

off into the woods. "It is good Captain Standish trained the men beforehand," Alice said, observing her husband disappear into the dark forest.

Carver motioned to them. "Come, ye must get down on the beach and ready to leave."

There was great confusion as the group was torn, some hurrying to get their children into the boat and others not wanting to leave the new found land.

"Will Father be safe?" Joseph asked Priscilla as they were placed in a boat just for children and young people on the second trip.

"Ye know he will," she answered quickly, trying to convince herself and trying not to show that it was the first time in her life that she had ever known this terrifying, piercing sensation of fear. It had not occurred to her before that anything dreadful might really happen to her father, her mother, or Joseph, or even herself. Now there was this possibility. She shivered as the cold wind blew across the water and looked longingly back at the shore where her mother stood waiting with the others for her chance to return to the *Mayflower*.

"We must attend to Carter," Priscilla told Joseph as they boarded. Not only, she told herself, was it her duty, but it would keep Joseph's mind busy until their mother came back on board—and her own, too.

Carter seemed to be sleeping, but fitfully. His face was very red, and Priscilla could feel that his fever was high when she touched his forehead. She took Joseph up on the main deck, hoping to find Alden. Going to portside to look ashore, she suddenly saw him on the deck above, leaning against the upper rail with his back to her, laughing and talking with Desire. She stayed a moment, and then took Joseph back below.

121

Her mother returned in the fifth boatload, and Joseph ran to her with a cry as she came down the companionway. After she had also checked Carter, the three of them went back above decks and huddled together in the lee of a bulwark to await Mullins's return. Alden and Desire had disappeared.

Brewster, Allerton, and Hopkins were also on deck, watching the fire on shore with several of the armed men silhouetted against it.

"Not a sign of them and no sound," Brewster said in a loud whisper.

"They've been gone for a long time now," Allerton added.

Stephen Hopkins went up the ladder for a better look. "At least there've been no musket shots."

"No time to fire, maybe," Allerton mumbled morosely.

Brewster shook his head. "Not with Standish in charge."

Suddenly there was activity near the fire. "They're back," someone on deck shouted. People appeared from below all at once to watch as the boat set out from shore.

When the scouting party pulled alongside and began climbing aboard, Brewster spoke meaningfully: "Thank God ye're safe."

"Did ye catch the Indian?" Allerton prodded the tired men, "or see any others?"

"We saw four of them," Standish asserted off-handedly. There was a gasp from the onlookers.

"Standish told them to halt . . . that we were friends," Bradford said wearily—but managed a hint of a smile as he looked at Brewster.

"But them Indians disappeared as quick as mice," Standish went on vigorously. "Ran up the beach and into the woods."

"We are glad ye have returned without harm." Brewster shook Standish's hand and squeezed his elbow.

"We must be armed at all times!" Standish called out loudly.

Brewster nodded his head in agreement. "Ye are right. We must be careful. But there is much work to be done, and, since these Indians do not have muskets, a few armed men may be sufficient."

The group broke up then, and Priscilla followed her family below decks. She was not ready yet to join the girls in the captain's cabin. She wanted to hear more about the scouting trip from her father and to find out whether Carter was better, but, also, she was afraid she might find Alden with Desire Minter.

After checking to see that nothing further could be done for Carter and that he was resting somewhat more peacefully, her parents returned to the family cubicle. Mullins was in a mood to talk, and he drew his family close about him, the three older ones sitting on stools and Joseph cross-legged at their feet. They held hands first in a short prayer of thanksgiving for their safe passage, and then her father gave special thanks for the beautiful land to which God had led them.

" 'Tis everything we could have wished for or dreamed about," he said animatedly. "There will be rich land for farming, and we will look over this lovely bay from whatever location we select and enjoy it from our farms and from our homes. There are fish in the streams and the bay, and game in the woods. The summer will be magnificent and fruitful.

"These people we are among are kind, diligent, wise, and God-fearing. We must be patient and humble for a while and bear our burdens with resignation and confidence in the Lord, for I fear it will be many weeks before we have adequate shelter on the land and with the weather and the condition of this ship and our provisions, we may have much discomfort and even suffering."

He rose. "Now I will go and watch over Carter tonight, and the rest of ye get a good night's sleep."

Priscilla returned to the cabin above and found all the girls asleep. She felt guilty for having had unkind thoughts about Desire and did not sleep well.

Next day she wondered whether her father had had a premonition, for that afternoon Carter died. He had been a good and faithful servant to them for many years. Not having any family of his own, he had practically adopted them and they, him. He had eaten with them, worked with them, and played with them. It was he who had first urged her father to "let the children come along" when they had gone fishing and hunting. It was deeply sorrowful for Priscilla and her parents, but for Joseph it was traumatic. It was his first experience with losing someone he loved. Priscilla had remained below with him during the services for Carter, trying to distract him by reading his favorite book, but he sat limply by her side, shaken by small sobs until she noticed he had fallen asleep from exhaustion, sitting straight up, his head against her shoulder.

After that, Joseph clung to his father with near hysteria whenever he left the ship to hunt for food with others on shore or on short scouting expeditions. Women and children were not allowed to leave the boat since the Indians had been sighted.

When the shallop was nearly finished, it was Alden's idea that Joseph should accompany him on its launching and try-out. Joseph was overjoyed, and he jumped about with excitement—but it pleased Priscilla more.

The day came when the long expedition to discover their new location was to be made. Provisions had been loaded into the shallop for three days. Priscilla, her mother, and brother were on deck when the men assembled in full armor.

Beside Mullins and John Alden, there were Bradford, Standish, and six of the passengers, the second mate Coppin, and two sailors.

Priscilla felt a sense of insecurity with her father, Alden, Bradford and Captain Standish all leaving, but she smiled and wished them all Godspeed with the others. Then, just as the boat was being lowered, Desire Minter ran up and pressed little muffins and sweetmeats into the hands of Alden, Howland, and the two Edwards, Dotey and Leister, and waved her handkerchief at them as they rowed away. The men on board laughed and chaffed Alden and the other three. Priscilla saw Alden turn his face away, and he did not look back at the *Mayflower* but pulled hard on the oars.

She spent the next week helping her mother care for the growing number of passengers who had become ill and trying to keep Joseph and the other children busy and contented. She and her mother strengthened each other with prayers and talking of the absent men.

Bradford would later describe the trip ashore in his journal:

> *On the 6th of December we set out in our shallop again with ten of our principal men, intending to circulate that deep bay of Cape Cod. The weather was very cold, and it froze so hard with the spray landing on our coats, they were as if glazed; yet that night we got down in the bottom of the boat, and, as we drew near the shore, we saw some ten or twelve Indians very busy about something. We landed about a league or two from them, and had much ado to put ashore anywhere, it lay so full of flats. Being landed, it grew late, and we made ourselves a barricade of logs and boughs as well as we could do in the time, and set out our sentinel and betook ourselves to rest, and saw the smoke of the fire the sav-*

ages made that night. When morning came, we divided our company, some to coast along the shore in the boat, and the rest to march through the woods to see the land, if there might be a fit dwelling place.

We came also to the place where we had seen the Indians before, and found they had been cutting up a great fish like a grampus, being some two inches thick of hide like a hog, some pieces whereof they had left by the way; and the shallop found two more of the fishes dead on the sand. So we ranged up and down all day, but found no people nor any place we liked. When the sun grew low, those of us on land hurried out of the woods to meet the shallop, which we did at high-water; of which we were very glad, for we had not seen each other since the morning. So we made a barricade as we did every night, with stakes and pine boughs, the height of a man, leaving it open to leeward, partly to shelter us from the cold and wind (making a fire in the center and lying around it), and partly to defend us from sudden assaults from the savages, if we should be surrounded. So being very weary, we took ourselves to rest. But about midnight we heard a hideous great cry, and our sentinel called—"Arm! Arm!"—so we stood to our arms and shot off a couple of muskets, and then the noise ceased. We concluded it was a company of wolves or such-like beasts, for one of the seamen had told us he had heard such a noise in Newfoundland. So we rested till about five o'clock in the morning.

So after prayer, we prepared for breakfast, and it being dawning, it was thought best to carry things down to the boat. Some said it was not best to carry the arms down; others said they would be the readier. But some three or four would not carry theirs till they went themselves, yet as it fell out, the water not being high enough, they laid them down on the bank, and came up for breakfast. But presently, all of a sudden, we heard a great and strange cry, which we knew to be the same as we had heard in the night, and one of our company came running in crying—"Men! Indi-

ans! Indians!"—and withal their arrows came flying among us. Our men ran with all speed to recover our arms, as by the good providence they did.

In the meantime, of those that were ready, two muskets were discharged at them, and two more stood ready at the entrance of our rendezvous, but were commanded not to shoot till they could take full aim at them; and the other two charged with all speed, for there were only four had arms there. The cry of the Indians was dreadful, especially when they saw our men run out of the rendezvous toward the shallop to recover their arms, the Indians wheeling about upon them. But some running out with coats of mail on, and cutlasses in their hands, they soon got their arms and let fly amongst the Indians and quickly stopped their violence.

Yet there was a lusty man, and no less valiant, stood behind a tree within half a musket shot, and let his arrows fly at us. He was seen to shoot three arrows which were all avoided. He stood three shots of our muskets, till one, taking full aim at him, made the bark and splinters fly about his ears, after which he gave an extraordinary shriek, and away they went, all of them.

We left some to keep the shallop, and followed them about a quarter of a mile, and shouted once or twice and shot two or three pieces and so returned. This we did that they might conceive that we were not afraid of them or in any way discouraged.

Thus it pleased God to vanquish our enemies, and give us deliverance; and by His special providence so to dispose that not any one of us was either hurt or hit, though their arrows came close by and on every side, and sundry of our coats, which hung up in the barricade, were shot through and through. Afterwards we gave God solemn thanks and gathered up a bundle of their arrows and called the place the First Encounter.

From hence we departed and coasted all along, but discerned no place likely for harbor, and therefore hasted to a place that our pilot, Mr. Coppin, assured us was a good harbor, which he had been in, and which we might reach before night, of which we were glad, for it began to be foul weather. After some hours of sailing, it began to snow and rain, and about the middle of the afternoon the wind increased and the sea became very rough, and we broke our rudder, and it was as much as two men could do to steer her with a couple of oars. But our pilot bade us be of good cheer, for he saw the harbor, but, the storm increasing and night drawing on, we bore what sail we could to get in while we could see. But herewith we broke our mast to three pieces and our sail fell overboard in a very green sea, so as we were like to be cast away, yet but by God's mercy we recovered ourselves and, having the flood with us, struck into the harbor.

But when we got there, our pilot said he had never seen this place before, and he would have run her ashore, and the Lord be merciful unto us for he would have run her into a cove full of breakers, before the wind. But he bade those who rowed, if they were men, about with the boat and turn her back, or else we were all cast away, and which they did with speed.

So he bade them be of good cheer and row lustily, for there was a fair Sound before them, and he doubted not we should find one place or other where we might ride in, safely. And though it was very dark and rained sore, yet in the end we got in the lee of a small island and remained there all that night in safety.

But we did not know this to be an island till morning. Some wanted to stay in the boat for fear they be amongst Indians; others were so weak with cold they could not endure, so went ashore, and with much ado built a fire (everything being so wet), and the rest were then glad to come to them, for after midnight the wind shifted and it froze hard. But though this had been a day and night of much danger to us, yet God gave us a morning of comfort and re-freshment (as He usually does to His children), for the next day was fair and sunshining. We found ourselves to be on an island se-cure from the Indians where we might dry our stuff, fix our pieces, *and rest and give God thanks for His mercies. And this being the last day of the week we prepared to keep the Sabbath.*

On Monday we sounded the harbor and found it fit for shipping, and marched inland and found diverse cornfields and little running brooks, a place fit for situation; at least it was the best we could find, with the season and our present necessity, and we were glad to accept it. So we returned toward the ship again to give them this good news which did comfort our hearts.

It was when the expedition party approached the *Mayflower* with jubilation, waving and shouting in greeting, that they found no answering exuberance on board or any sign from any of the passengers, and only after they had come aboard did they learn that Dorothy Bradford had fallen overboard and drowned.

Chapter Twelve

Dorothy Bradford's death had brought a strange silence to the ship. Everyone aboard, including the sailors, mourned. They became as one family and treated each other with deep-felt courtesy and kindness day in and day out.

William Bradford was respected and admired by all. Now he lay on his pallet, not speaking and running a high fever.

Priscilla asked herself over and over what she could have done. Had Dorothy really just *fallen* overboard? Where had everyone failed her? Had she herself been too busy with her own thoughts and the activities of daily living to seek out Dorothy and get her to talk about her problems? . . . for Priscilla felt sure the tragedy had not been an accident. Although her father assured her that sometimes people who are the most desperate hide their problems very well, Priscilla felt that she should have spent more time with Dorothy.

Mrs. White had been the last one to see Dorothy, helping her tie a scarf about her shoulders—the same one that had been found floating four hours later. Alice Mullins, needing some special floss, had sent Priscilla to look for Dorothy when she was not in the Bradford cubicle. Priscilla had looked all over the ship to no avail, and began to be alarmed when no one seemed to have seen her. It was Alice who had gone to the captain finally, and he had immediately put the ship's shore boat down and had his sailors search for her. Since the *Mayflower* was far offshore, there was no chance she could have reached land. And then one of the sailors had found the scarf.

There seemed to be no consoling Bradford. Those close to him feared he might take his own life or succumb to the general illness, for he was often delirious. Alice felt the exposure on the expedition had weakened him, and the tragedy had destroyed his great gift of leadership.

Yet Elder Brewster, even in his own grief for Dorothy, told Governor Carver to proceed with plans for moving the ship to the new harbor.

On the 15th day of December they weighed anchor to go to the place that had been chosen for their settlement. Once more the *Mayflower* was under sail and once more a storm came up that rendered it impossible to get into the harbor. On December 16th, however, it was fair, and the ship found safe haven at last.

Everyone went ashore. They surveyed the land eagerly and carefully, judging its potential of safety, food, and warmth, and realizing its stark, unspoiled beauty.

Brewster gathered them all together and spoke to them.

"Come everyone, let us join for a moment of meditation." He placed his Bible on a nearby large stone. "Gather 'round this rock, all of you. Let us kneel." Mullins, Standish, and the men in armor bent with difficulty. All except a few of the sailors knelt in the snow and cold. The only sounds came from the children playing on the beach.

"Even as the Lord told Simon Peter . . . 'upon this rock I will found my Church' . . . so let this stone be a symbol to us of our determination to build here in this country a colony based upon love and kindness . . . the divine principles of our Lord God and Jesus Christ, with each man free to worship Him in his own spirit. Give us courage to meet the trials we must face with patience, love, and dedication, knowing that every deed of charity and fortitude will be remembered by Thee, Lord, when we meet face to face. Let us truly love one another as we undertake this new venture, and bless each one of us, O mighty God, and bless these sailors who have brought us to our destination. Be our fortress and our strength in this place we shall call Plymouth Plantation. Amen."

The pilgrims rose silently to their feet, looking around them in full realization of the occasion. William and Alice Mullins held hands and put arms around their children.

"This is what I dreamed of," Mullins smiled happily, in spite of the cold and hoarseness that plagued him ever since the scouting expedition. He surveyed the tall, waving grasses on the beach, the flat area slightly above it, and the wooded hill behind it to the west. "The spring will be beautiful here . . . with the trees, the fields for planting, the running streams and the harbor . . . we have everything we could possibly want. It is a good place. It is home."

Priscilla, noticing that Alden was busy with the governor and others as they walked about with a large scroll of plans, discussing locations for the village to be, went with her family as they looked about.

Her father showed them the location that had been nearly settled upon for a large Common House. "This will be the first shelter to be constructed . . . a house for God . . . a log house for the sick and the children and their mothers. It will not be easy nor fast in this bitter weather," he said regretfully, "but the men will begin felling trees and digging foundations tomorrow."

The thought of it sent a thrill through Priscilla, and Joseph jerked impatiently at his father's arm. "Can I watch?" he pleaded. "Can I?"

Mullins laughed. "We will see," he equivocated.

By the time Priscilla had dressed and eaten with the girls in the captain's cabin the next morning, she found that many of the men, including Alden, had already gone ashore to begin work. Her father, however, was still with his family. He was pale and shaking with chills but refused to lie down despite his wife's urgent pleas. "I should be out there with the rest," he fumed. "There is so much work to do and who knows how long the captain will keep his ship here."

It was all Priscilla and her mother could do to keep him with them. Priscilla fetched water from their barrel, made some tea and porridge for the family, and for Bradford, too, and took it below. Joseph was loathe to leave his father, but Priscilla took him with her, and he soon joined in the games the boys were playing on deck.

The young girls were busy making quilts for the Common House to be used for the sick, and Priscilla joined them in the captain's cabin. It was so very cold as she watched the boys playing from the poop deck that she wondered if she should have let Joseph be outside, after all.

For the noon meal she warmed some of the fish soup from the night before. As night approached, her mother finally succeeded in getting her father to lie down on his pallet. Priscilla again did the cooking in the icy wind, sharing the fire with Elizabeth Hopkins and Mary Brewster. They took turns going out to tend the rabbits that the men had caught on the expedition.

It was later that night, after the evening meal, that she crossed the deck to return to the captain's cabin. She noticed the wind had died down. Her father had begun to run a high fever, and she had wanted to stay below to help her mother, but Alice had urged her to get a good sleep so that she could be of help on the morrow.

As Priscilla climbed the ladder to the sterncastle, she saw that a heavy fog was gathering. The deck seemed deserted, and the lanterns fore and aft gave off an eerie light. She was about to go into the cabin when she heard muffled laughter. In the dim light she saw someone with John Alden, standing near a bulwark below. Not wanting him to think she was eavesdropping, she quickly stepped around the corner.

"Oh, Mister Alden . . . John." It was Desire's voice. "All the girls think ye are . . . attractive! Ye are the talk of the captain's cabin. Priscilla especially."

Alden said something inaudible.

"Well, I'd never do that," Desire went on. "I think ye are much too handsome . . . too strong, too. . . ." Priscilla couldn't catch the rest of it. There was a silence. "Oh, ye are wonderful, John," she heard Desire sigh.

Then: "Ye are really a mischievous little wench." Alden's voice was loud and clear. Another silence. "Come on," he said, after a minute, "that's enough of this. Ye must go on up. The captain'll have me flogged if he catches us, and your father will have me thrown overboard."

"Oh, they'd never do that to ye, and ye know it." Desire laughed, and then there was no sound again.

Priscilla, unable to resist temptation, peeked around the corner just as Desire threw her arms around Alden's neck and, drawing his head down, kissed him eagerly on the mouth.

Alden held her a minute, then gently pulled her arms away. "I must go now. I have work to do."

But Desire kissed him again, and this time John did not resist but held her close.

Priscilla couldn't watch any more. She stepped back toward the cabin door as softly as possible and slipped inside just as the girls were blowing out the candles. Quickly she undid her dress and petticoat and put on her nightdress. She had hardly gotten into the hammock when Desire entered, humming a little tune.

All night Priscilla lay awake, turning in anger one minute and in self-pity the next. She tried to remind herself that this was not a proper way of thinking and finally calmed herself by recalling Bible verses. "Love suffereth long, and is kind; love envieth not; love vaunteth not itself, doth not behave itself unseemly, seeketh not her own, is not provoked, thinketh no evil. . . ." Ah, that was it . . . she must *not* be angry. She had no right—but she heard the ship's bell strike every hour until dawn, listened to the men boarding boats for work on shore, and even thought she heard John Alden's voice.

As soon as possible Priscilla rose and dressed, trying not to disturb the others. She looked at Desire, sleeping quietly, a smile on her lips. Then she hurried out the door, down the ladder, and on toward the main cabin. As she went, all thought of the scene the night before faded like a bad dream. She could only feel the urgency to be near her father.

From the top of the companionway she could see there was trouble. Her mother, the doctor, Joseph, and Mrs. Brewster were gathered around the pallet on which her father lay, gasping for breath. Even as she hurried toward them, others were awakening and looking out in alarm. They stepped back to let Priscilla through. Her mother turned, putting her arm around Priscilla.

Alice spoke as if in a stupor. "He seemed to be sleeping quietly. I sat beside him until after midnight. We were talking, and he was breathing easily, so I went to sleep. Suddenly I wakened. He was shaking and delirious. He began gasping, and I covered him with blankets. It did no good. Ye can see how he is, raging with fever, unconscious except when he gasps." Alice wrung her hands in desperation, the tears streaming down her face.

The doctor massaged her father's chest, trying to clear the lungs. It was then that Priscilla noticed Joseph. He was stark white, eyes wide, speechless, and not moving. Priscilla bent down and took him in her arms.

"Take him away," her mother said. "Priscilla, take him on deck!"

Priscilla knew her mother did not want them to see their father die.

"But Mama . . . ?"

"You stay with him, Priscilla!"

She did not want to go, but she led Joseph through the group and up on deck. She looked around for someone to care for Joseph, but there was no one. She paced back and forth, unable to believe this could be happening.

Joseph clutched her hand tightly, shivering. "Is Papa going to die?" he whispered, his innocent face looking up at her.

"I don't know, Joseph, I just don't know," she answered honestly.

Mary Brewster came on deck and took Joseph's hand.

"Is he . . . ?" Priscilla asked, choking on the unsaid word.

Mary shook her head, looking away, not answering.

Coming down the companionway Priscilla could see Elder Brewster. She joined her mother, kneeling beside her father. There was complete silence except for his terrible gasping. Then, suddenly, he was gone.

Alice and Priscilla clung tightly to each other. In the stillness Priscilla heard the elder's voice. "When we feel the raging storms around us, touch our lives," he prayed. "Let us know that Ye are near, sustaining us, supporting us with Thy strength and with Thine ever-present love. Bless our brave, wise friend and receive him in the wondrous new world of Thy heaven. His spirit will always be with us. Amen."

Priscilla studied the face of her dear, dead father. They had understood each other—had been so much alike. Was it only last night they had been talking together? Making plans for the future? Now today seemed so full of terror.

She looked up to see John Alden, a stricken look on his face. She looked away. It was all a blur—a dream. Then they were taking her father away—John Alden and some others. She knew she was becoming hysterical, but she reached out with a cry. Alice put her hand on Priscilla's arm, and the touch brought her back to reality. It was she who should be consoling her mother. Priscilla pulled herself up straight, composed herself, and took her mother's hand.

With Joseph lying between them that night, Priscilla did not allow herself to cry, but she heard her mother's strangled sobs.

Her father was the first one to be buried on the hill. Her mother had chosen John Alden to be one of the pallbearers. He approached Priscilla in passing. "I'm so sorry . . . ," he began. She only looked at him calmly, unsmiling. "Thank ye," she'd said and walked away. In her grief she felt nothing for him.

Elder Brewster held the services, speaking of his and her father's long friendship and of the man of wisdom and benevolence and courage that William Mullins had been. The ground was frozen hard, and the grave was not very deep.

Chapter Thirteen

By Christmas Day sills had been laid for the Common House, and services were held there. It was a solemn occasion. Four more pilgrims had died from exposure and one sailor. Captain Jones stood behind Elder Brewster and at one point thanked the assembled group "for their Christian love in taking the risk and remedying my men, too."

Priscilla and her mother had thrown themselves into caring for the ill and especially for William Bradford. His fever was subsiding, but very slowly. All the men and even some of the women worked together on building the Common House. Once, when crossing the beach, Priscilla had passed John Alden. She'd attempted to hurry by, but he had caught her arm. "Priscilla, I must speak with ye. What is wrong?" he had demanded. "Nothing. Nothing at all."—and she'd pulled her arm away and walked off. Afterward she was sorry. It was a stupid thing to have done.

Alden had tried twice more to get Priscilla to speak with him alone, but she just couldn't bring herself to do it. After all, what could she say? How could she begin? Now for the last three weeks he had avoided her, also.

By the end of January, fourteen of their group had died and only seven of the men had escaped the malady. The Common House had been finished nevertheless and was now filled with people down with the sickness.

Captain Standish had ordered that burials be at night in unmarked graves. Although they had not been bothered by Indians, Indians had been seen in the distance from time to time. Standish did not think it wise to let them know how many had been lost from their group.

With so many men ill and unable to hunt, there was a great scarcity of food. Priscilla had overheard John Crackston who, with his son was sick abed, saying: "My little John is so hungry he can't cry any more . . . just whimper."

"What we need is meat!" Edward Winslow said from his pallet. "But with the snow so deep and none to hunt . . . we can't go on with just weevily biscuits. Even what's left of the beer has been taken over by the sailors. They will give us none . . . even for our sick."

"If we could only get two or three big bucks . . . that would keep us a week or more," Crackston sighed.

Even though it was snowing, Priscilla had resolved to do something about the situation. There had been a hunting party going out the next morning, and Priscilla had decided to join it. That night she presented the idea to Mary Chilton, who had also lost her father. In the morning the girls appeared at dawn to join Miles Standish, John Alden, Gilbert Winslow, and Peter Browne. They heard Peter Browne as they approached.

"I can't be seeing right," he was muttering. "It looks like . . . it can't be. Mistress Priscilla and Mistress Chilton . . . *wearing men's clothes!*"

"Good morning," Priscilla said firmly, "and please don't be startled. What we are wearing may not be usual . . . but, if we are to go hunting, our skirts would catch on the underbrush. We intend to get food for the sick. There aren't enough of the men to bring in sufficient game for all sixty-eight of us."

John Alden gasped. "Hunting! This is folly. There is no place on this foray for women. It is much too dangerous. Ye would probably wind up shooting each other and one of us."

"Just one moment," Standish broke in with a sharp, commanding tone. "These brave young women have been studying to handle their fathers' muskets with me. They have learned the art of weaponry quite well . . . and also the orders of the hunt. I see no reason why they should not join us. I, myself, will accompany them."

"But surely ye can't allow women . . . !" Alden sputtered. "Besides, there might be Indians."

"We have encountered none such," Standish asserted as if he were addressing a child. "And if one should appear, I shall handle the matter promptly. Come, ladies," he said, and proceeded into the forest.

After Priscilla had passed Alden, she allowed herself the first smile since her father had died.

Under Standish's directions Priscilla thought the three of them—Standish, Mary, and herself—did quite well. They returned to the Common House with a deer Standish had shot, five rabbits, and a fox that might not be good for food but whose pelt was most useful. There were two more deer the others had gotten, several rabbits, and Alden had shot a bear. This meat was considered a delicacy as well as necessary food.

The other men congratulated the girls on their achievements, but Alden turned on his heel and walked away.

After helping the men to store the catch prior to preparation, Priscilla went into the Common House to see her mother. She was bending over William Bradford.

"It is dreadful that I lie here while women are forced to do a man's work," he spoke with dismay. "It is time I rise and take on my duties."

"Do not fret thyself, Master Bradford," Priscilla said, bending beside him. "I did not mind the hunting as long as it was for necessary food. It is very satisfying to be able to assist in feeding the hungry, and the trek through the woods was quite invigorating."

Bradford looked at her flushed cheeks and bright eyes. "Indeed, ye do look cheery and winsome, and I suppose ye should be congratulated for thy prowess as a huntress."

"That is more than I deserve . . . but thanks."

"I intend to be up tomorrow in spite of thy mother's solicitation. The two of ye have brought me back to life . . . a life I did not care to live for a long while."

"We shall be glad to have thee back for ye have been sorely missed," Priscilla answered with a smile and was surprised to discover that she had used the intimate pronoun.

Not only Priscilla and Alice but all the women and men who were well spent much of their time caring for their poor patients. Life began to be a horror. Not a week passed without two or three more deaths, among them Rose Standish and Catherine Carver. Nor was the Common House a good place for those with difficulty in breathing, something those with the illness usually manifested. A hole had been left in the roof for the smoke from their heating fire to escape. It not only was drafty, but the room was often acrid with fumes. Once the makeshift roof caught on fire, and the ill had to be moved outside in the freezing weather.

Every sign of a cough or sneeze from those still well was regarded with terror. Joseph had been perfectly well when they had put him to bed one night. Around midnight he had wakened his mother. His teeth were chattering, and he was shaking from head to foot. Held close to his mother with all the quilts and clothing Priscilla had piled on top of them, he continued to shake.

Priscilla could feel the terrible height of his fever by feeling his forehead. She and her mother and the doctor did everything possible, but after two more days little Joseph died.

Afterward, for nearly two weeks, Priscilla feared for her mother's sanity. In the beginning Alice had sobbed and moaned and paced about constantly in a way Priscilla had not thought possible for her well-controlled mother. Alice remained constantly on the cold, damp ship, eating practically nothing. She was becoming extremely haggard-looking. Priscilla would find her many times on deck in the middle of the night in her nightdress, staring out to sea, as if she cared no more for life.

"Mama, I am still here, and I am thy daughter," she felt forced to say, for her mother's own good. And, in truth, Priscilla did begin to feel abandoned for she, too, grieved for her loved ones.

It was only when Alice became ill with the fever herself that her behavior returned to normal. It was as if she were doing penance for some misdeed and was contented with the pain of it—Alice, who had only cared and worked for her family all her life. Alice Mullins was taken ashore to the Common House where Priscilla remained with her night and day. She shut everyone out of her life except Elder Brewster.

One night Priscilla briefly left the confines of the Common House and went outside to watch the heavy snowfall and breathe some fresh air. As she opened the door to go back inside, she stopped a moment, surveying the dismal scene. On the dirt floor around the low-burning fire the sick were lying on straw pallets supported by sacked tree twigs. Candles were glowing here and there, lighting the faces of the patients, some of them moaning, some sleeping, some praying. The draft from the door blew the smoke around the room, and Priscilla quickly shut it.

She did not see Alden and Standish at the far end of the room in the corner. She dusted the snow off her clothes, lighted a candle, and made her way through the patients to her mother. Alice was lying, eyes wide open, lips moving in silent prayer.

"Mama, are thee still awake? Thee should try to rest."

"I cannot sleep for thinking of Joseph and my poor husband."

"I know, dear . . . but they do not need thee now as much as I do. Thee must save thy strength for both of us."

There was a silence. Finally her mother whispered: "I know that well, Priscilla. Ye are the dearest daughter any mother could ever wish for. Ye are thoughtful of everyone and gentle and good . . . but underneath there is a certain fortitude I have seen. I know ye will find it, should it become necessary . . . and in this hard land it probably will. It is a beautiful place, though, with a good life well worth striving for. Ye are young, and will find thy happiness, I know."

"Mother," Priscilla protested, "I will not hear this talk. Thee must save thy strength. . . ."

"No, I have lived a long, full life . . . with my own certain joys. I am tired now. I cannot live without all my family. If ye grieve too much, ye will cause me sorrow, wherever I may be. Just remember our good days together." Alice managed a smile. "If God wills, I will wait for thee to join us. May it be a long time for thee."

"Mother. Mother." Priscilla made no effort to stop the tears. "I cannot go on without thee . . . without anyone."

Alice tried to sit up, summoning her courage and breathing with difficulty. "Yes thee can, Priscilla. Remember, when grief or loneliness overwhelms thee, throw thyself into work for the Lord. There is so much to be done . . . the other bereaved, the ill, the children."

"Nothing could console me, Mama."

Alice lay back on the pallet, exhausted. "Ye will never be alone, if ye pray. Now, my dear darling, go back to Mary

Brewster. She will care for thee and guide thee. I will sleep peacefully now. Always know, wherever I am, I will be with thee, my love."

Priscilla embraced her mother, her face wet. Then she rose and hurried from the Common House. As she threw open the door, John Alden stepped beside her, catching her arm. "Let me go with thee."

Not wanting anyone's sympathy, she pulled away and fled out into the snowstorm. As she walked to the beach along the half-hidden path, the flakes began to cool her face and the softness of them to soothe her. She stood still in the gray silence, finding her breath again. When she turned to go back, she found Alden and Standish had been walking quietly behind her. Priscilla did not speak, nor did they.

She returned to her mother's side. Presently Mary and William Brewster joined her, watching with her and comforting her as her mother died.

So once again Priscilla went to the burial ground where her father and brother had been buried and now where her mother would lie. Although the graves were not marked, they were well-fixed in her mind, and she had taken care that her mother be buried next to her loved ones. Again the funeral had to be at night.

The ceremony was short so as not to attract attention. Alden, Standish, Allerton, and Edward Winslow carried her mother. Brewster bowed his head to the darkness, holding the one candle that had lighted the way. "In the name of the Father, the Son, and the Holy Ghost, Amen. We commend this the soul of our dear dead departed one to Thy care, O Lord. May she find the joy with Thee that she so well earned on earth. And bless us all, too, who loved her, that we may carry on as she would wish. Amen."

In spite of her mother's wishes, Priscilla returned to her

family's area aboard ship. She politely refused everyone's kind offers to eat with them and shunned everyone's efforts to console her. She was afraid of meeting people, of having to speak, of being touched. She became very thin, eating only the tidbits she found in the cubicle.

She had never imagined anything so terrible could happen to her family—least of all to little Joseph—or herself. She was frightened—not so much of dying as of loneliness. She felt so starkly alone—an alien in a strange land—lost—hearing strange voices—her mother's, Carter's—jumping at sounds, of a sudden creak in the hull, of a cry from the deck, of rats scratching on the floor. She lay on the pallet, covering her head with pillows if anyone came near.

Several days later, unable to stand the night's silence and the fetid, suffocating air, Priscilla went up on deck. There was a bright moon, and she went to the far rail, leaning on it and watching the quicksilver dancing of ripples on the water. She was startled by someone coming up behind her and looked around to find John Alden standing there. Priscilla turned back, not speaking, and he came up to the rail and stood beside her, silently watching the water with her. Presently he spoke, very softly.

"I, too, lost all my family," he said. "I ran away in my desperation, but it did me no good. I have no home, nor town, nor relatives, nor friends. I am alone. It is not good to be alone, Priscilla. Ye cannot cut thyself off from life, especially not here. And there are those who need ye . . . very much."

In her distress Priscilla could not answer, and after a minute he left. It began to grow quite cold, and clouds scudded across the moon. At last she drew her cape around her and walked slowly back to the companionway. As she started down the steps, she saw Alden, watching her from the deck above.

She no longer felt any rancor toward him, or toward Desire, either. It was wrong of her to have been so upset. She could see that now. And it was kind of him to have sought her out.

Little by little she tried to force herself out of the cubicle, although each step was terrifying. She didn't speak to anyone except to thank them when they brought her food. She realized they understood, also, in their own grief, and respected her wish to be alone. Yet she was aware of their encouragement—Mary Brewster, John Alden, Miles Standish, Constance, Mary Chilton—even Desire.

A few days later there was much commotion on the deck above, and she heard weeping and moaning. She went to the foot of the companionway and overheard that Governor Carver had taken sick while planting in the field and had suddenly died three hours later. There was consternation and grief all around Priscilla. It was as if the loss of this wise leader was more than the group could endure, as if all the terrors of the sea—the cold, the hunger, the suffering, and the sorrow—had all been in vain.

The day after the governor's death, no one left the ship. The communal strength seemed to have crumbled. People passed each other silently or gathered in clusters, eyes downcast, hardly speaking.

Priscilla began to think of the sick left ashore in the Common House. She remembered her mother's words, and Alden's, and, making an effort, she rose and left the cubicle and went up on deck in the daylight.

It was strange to find the ship so uncrowded. The loss of each person had been of such concern that the cumulative effect of so many deaths had not struck Priscilla as much as now. There were groups about, to be sure. Desire was with Constance Hopkins and the two young men, Edward Dotey and Edward Leister, talking at the rail. Some of the men, Allerton, Howland, the Winslows, and Peter Browne were standing by the ladder. The Billington boys and some of the other children were sitting on the deck, playing quietly. Priscilla instinctively looked for Joseph, then caught herself. John was not on deck, nor were any of the other girls from the captain's cabin. She had heard that Mary Chilton had also lost her mother and Elizabeth Tilley had lost both her parents and her aunt and uncle. It was, indeed, a sad time for them all. Priscilla found a sailor and asked to be rowed ashore.

It was as she suspected. Only Mary Brewster, the good doctor who had lost his wife Ann a few weeks before, and young Mrs. Hopkins were there to give aid in the Common House. And twenty-year-old Susanna White, who had lost her husband two weeks before, was giving birth. Elizabeth Hopkins was comforting Susanna, whose labor was becoming more and more difficult.

Mary Brewster, welcoming Priscilla with a smile and a kiss, put her to work immediately caring for five-year-old Resolved White, fetching water from the spring and heating it, cooking for the other patients, bathing the women and children, and getting wood for the fire.

As night came, Susanna gave birth to another son, and there was joy as Mary carried him around for the other patients to see—the first cheer to come to that room since it had been built. Elder Brewster, coming in after the formal burial services for the governor, gave his benediction.

Priscilla worked until she ached with fatigue and then fell asleep on one of the pallets in the Common House. She continued on through the week, helping Mary Brewster with the patients and caring for the ten motherless children. Gradually she persuaded the other girls, including Desire, who had now lost both Governor Carver and his wife, to put aside

147

their grief and help, also.

Aboard the *Mayflower* it was apparent that a new governor was needed—someone of strong character who could assist Elder Brewster in renewing the Pilgrims' determination to build their colony—someone who was capable of attending to the many trying demands of organizing it and its people.

Bradford was the man selected, and the vote for him was unanimous. Brewster was especially pleased, but felt Bradford might need persuading. Priscilla, he said, was the one who might convince him.

At first she was reluctant to attempt such a serious undertaking, but Brewster assured her Bradford would be more receptive to her suggestion than to anyone else's.

Bradford was pale and shaky but able to walk a little, and Priscilla carried a bench outside as it was sunny. "Here we can have some privacy," she said, "for I have been appointed to discuss a very serious question with thee."

He looked at her curiously.

She started out by saying that she was happy to see he was recovering so well. "We have all missed thy guidance," she added.

"Ye may come directly to thy question," Bradford said firmly, "for I am accustomed to grievous tidings."

"Oh, no," she added hastily, fearing she had begun badly. What if she should fail in this mission? Everyone would blame her. "It's not bad news at all. In fact, very good news . . . that is for us, I mean . . . that is, if ye will accept." Priscilla felt herself blushing as she looked at the man's puzzled face. She took a breath. "Mister Bradford, sir," she began more formally, "if ye agree, and if . . . no . . . *when* ye feel able . . . our people would like ye to be our new governor." She hurried on as he turned his face away. "The vote was unanimous."

"Although I am greatly honored," he said, after a moment,

"I do not feel worthy of this office. No one can take the governor's place. We are all forlorn and bereft of hope. I am not the one to restore that hope."

"I understand how ye feel," Priscilla answered more calmly. "Sometimes one cannot help wondering whether the Lord even knows where we are . . . this is such a lonely part of the world." Priscilla's voice started to break, then she went on quietly. "But ye are the one to restore that hope, if anyone can. Ye and Elder Brewster . . . and ye cannot put the burden on him alone. We must rediscover our mission, our goals, and our desires . . . or we are all sure to perish. We cannot go back to England . . . there is nothing to go back to. We must stay here and endure. Ye are the one chosen to guide us in accomplishing that."

"But will the company respect me? I am only thirty years old."

"There are very few left that are older than thee thyself now. And ye have the vision, the wisdom, and the authority that has earned the respect of the community."

"And do ye really believe I have all these things, Priscilla?"

"Yes, I have faith in thee, dear Mister Bradford."

He was silent, thinking. Then he took her hand. "If *ye* believe it, then I will accept."

She smiled. "I know ye can lead us into God's good grace."

"I will surely try. We are fortunate and blessed that Elder Brewster has been spared to us. He will help us overcome our many griefs."

On Sunday, Brewster gathered the members of the group into the Common House for prayer meeting. Of those left, twenty were men and boys over fourteen, eight were women and girls over fourteen, and twenty-two were children under fourteen.

149

Elder Brewster called Bradford to stand beside him. "We are proud and happy to greet as our new governor, William Bradford, who will guide us in bringing our dreams of a community founded on freedom, good will, and dedication to our Lord to realization. Bradford, my son, we welcome thee." Elder Brewster embraced him.

The group answered—"Amen."—with nods of satisfaction, except for John Billington, who had become testy of late, and declined with a loud groan. Brewster ignored him and, after a pause, went on in a different manner.

"Ye, my dear friends, who have been so courageous through many trials and much anguish have troubled me of late. We have all suffered, perhaps ye more than I. Yet we must remember that even though we walk through the valley of the shadow of death, we will fear no evil. It is the Lord's will. The Lord's rod and His staff will comfort us. We are not alone. The Lord *is* with us. If we are all not to perish, we must find our *faith* once more and return to our work as our strength will allow us. We will never forget those we have loved and lost, but we must not give in to discouragement and dismay.

"I believe there are signs that we are past this valley of death, for we have had no more leave us this last ten days and no new sick ones. We cannot give up now. Our dead have not died in vain. For them we carry on. Faith is everything.

"Let us leave all doubts behind. The Lord is with us now, as always. Let us forge our faith and with such strength and love that we will never again doubt our purpose . . . for it is God's will!"

The people waited quietly for a minute, and then there was a loud answer of—"Amen."

"We must *build* . . . build this colony into a frontier of freedom . . . an example before God that people *can* live together in peace, even as we, a mixed group, have learned to live together with love and forbearance. There is a footing laid for the first home in our village, that has been abandoned for over a month now. Let us start work on this building again as a cornerstone for a town worthy of the Lord."

A hymn was sung. The benediction was given, and, as the members left the Common House, they greeted each other and clung together as if they were all one family.

Priscilla even managed a restrained smile for John Alden as she passed, in answer to his helpless look.

Chapter Fourteen

It was not easy carrying out the good intentions of the Sabbath. The baby Oceanus Hopkins died amid community mourning. Only the settlers' feeling of closeness and support for each other enabled them to carry on. There were only twelve men left, but enough to do the heavy work of felling the trees, dragging them to the proper place, splitting them, and hoisting them into position. Alden labored ceaselessly, seeming to be everywhere at once. Bradford and Brewster were supervising. Standish was on guard.

Only John Billington refused to work. There were rumors that he was planning to move elsewhere, and that he was trying to stir up resentment against the original Separatists to get as many as possible to go with him. He remained on the ship, trying to make friends with the captain and arrange for passage farther south. His wife, however, wanted to be with the other women but had been forbidden to do so by her husband. Consequently she invented all kinds of excuses to go ashore and loudly bemoaned her fate. Her children, meanwhile, got into all kinds of mischief, and Billington himself was nearly hit by a heavy loose log that had rolled down the hill.

As the Common House gradually lost its patients, the *Mayflower* shore boat and the shallop began making many trips back and forth to the beach with the furniture and goods of the Pilgrims. The first sunny, warm day in March, a harbinger of spring, found almost the entire company ashore—Pilgrims, the captain, the sailors, and even John

Billington. Now everyone was working.

Mary Chilton had found three crocuses growing through the snow and had called Priscilla and Constance Hopkins away from spreading the washed clothes to dry on the bushes to see them. Children were playing hide-and-seek in the tall shore grasses. Men were carrying furniture up from the beach, and Standish had been called over to aid them. There was a great racket of noise from the saws and shouting back and forth. Suddenly there was a scream from one of the women.

An Indian stood silently and proudly in their midst, arms crossed. Panic spread among the people. Women ran shrieking after their children; men ran for their guns; the girls shrank closer together.

Brewster and Bradford stayed calm. They jumped atop a log and commanded the group to silence. It was as if the company turned instantly into statues, being reminded by their leaders to remain peaceful. Women stopped in mid-flight. Men hesitated, axes in mid-air. Children's heads popped out of the grass to watch. Every face was turned toward the Indian.

"Good day," the man said in plain English.

Abruptly there was confusion again. Settlers looked at each other as if those on the Tower of Babel had returned to speaking one language. There were loud murmurs.

"Did ye hear him?"

"What does he mean?"

"Who may he be?"

Again Elder Brewster called for calm. "Silence! Let us hear what he has to say."

"Friends! Welcome! Peace!" the Indian continued.

"It's a trap! Watch out!" John Billington yelled.

Everyone looked fearfully around, but there were no more

Indians to be seen. Nevertheless, Standish put his firing piece on the tripod and aimed it directly at the Indian who stood surveying him calmly.

"Standish," Brewster ordered. "Lower thy musket. Don't ye see that he is not armed? This is our first chance to make friends . . . what we've been waiting for."

"My name Samoset. Friend. You got biscuits, beads, beer?" The Indian stepped up toward Brewster.

"Yes. Would you like some?"

"Good. You know Squanto?"

"Squanto. Is that thy tribe? I have never heard of it," Bradford said.

"Not tribe. Squanto friend. He speak English better."

Brewster looked at him curiously. "How did ye learn to speak English?"

"I learn from sailors . . . your brother . . . Dermer."

Captain Jones's face lit up. "Dermer. Sure. Captain Dermer . . . explored along here. He made some charts."

"Yes . . . Captain Dermer. I help."

Brewster stepped down off the log, holding out his hand. "Welcome. We are glad ye came to us."

The Indian took Brewster's hand.

"Bring him food and drink," the captain kindly ordered as he nodded to Howland and one of the sailors.

Alden stepped forward. "Where is the rest of your tribe?"

"I not this tribe." He motioned to the land around. "Wampanoag this tribe. Live here. Get sick. Spirits go. All die. Only Squanto live. I with Massasoit. Nauset tribe. Him chief."

"Can we meet your chief?" Bradford asked.

"Squanto speak for Massasoit. He tell Massasoit."

"Where can we meet this Squanto?" Brewster said.

"He not far . . . he wait . . . see if you bring evil spirits. Me go!"

The Indian suddenly left.

Brewster called after him. "Some of our men will go with ye . . . "—but he had disappeared.

Standish stepped forward, weapon in hand. "I should not let him slip by. Do ye want me to go after him?"

Brewster regarded him pleasantly. "Miles, ye are a fine guardian for all of us. Do not fret. He has just gone to get his friend. He will be back."

After a moment Samoset returned with a tall, regal-looking Indian and four braves. The Pilgrims fell back apprehensively as the six Indians approached Brewster. They opened a sack they were carrying and laid it on the ground. It contained some tools they had stolen. Then the tall Indian bowed.

"*Señores. Señoras,*" he said. "Welcome, friends. My chief sends greetings. I speak Spanish and English as well as Indian language. I will be your friend."

"He is Squanto," Samoset proudly announced.

"We, too, wish to be your friends," Brewster responded. "Send our good wishes to your chief, also. We have gifts for him." He turned to Winslow and Allerton. "Please see that more jewelry, wine, beer, and biscuits are brought from the *Mayflower* for Chief Massasoit." Then he turned back to Squanto. "I want ye to understand how welcome ye and your tribe are here."

"How did ye learn to speak such excellent English?" Bradford asked.

Squanto regarded the group with quiet poise. "*Señor,*" he said, "I was stolen with four braves by Captain Hunt. He sell us as slaves in Spain. I escape to England where my good Master Brown teach me English. I have tutor. Captain Dermer bring me back to my people, but they all dead . . . gone. So I go to Nauset tribe."

"Please make it plain to your chief that we will harm no

one . . . that we will return the corn we have taken," Brewster said.

"Keep corn. We have plenty. I will help plant." Squanto pointed to the sack. "We have returned tools we take."

"Thank ye," Bradford told him. "We need these tools to build our houses."

"We do not need." Squanto spoke somewhat disdainfully. "We have wigwam."

"Tell your chief we will have peace between us," Brewster assured.

"I will tell him you friends."

"We should have an agreement . . . written, if possible." Alden spoke. He had come forward. "Our guns will be a protection for Massasoit . . . and we certainly need *his* help."

"He is quite right," Brewster went on to Squanto. "Can ye explain a peace treaty to him? It will be a defense for your chief against the other tribes and a safeguard for us."

"He know peace," Squanto spoke proudly. "We smoke peace pipe. I will call Massasoit."

Winslow and Allerton had returned with the gifts for the Indians, and Brewster and Bradford presented them to Samoset and Squanto.

The Indians then ceremoniously left, Squanto bowing in the continental fashion.

As he watched them disappear into the forest, Brewster announced: "They are a proud tribe. This is as it should be . . . for our mutual benefit." And then more soberly he added: "And the disease that wiped the Wampanoags out . . . it probably kept us from being attacked when we first landed"—and then he whispered as if to himself—"and perhaps is why so many of us have suffered and been lost. . . ."

The work in the village progressed and three cabins were

in the building. A large field had been cleared, and, as the weather grew warmer, the colonists planted their wheat and peas from the seeds they had brought. Squanto taught them how to plant corn, planting a dead fish beside each seed. The Pilgrims' fish hooks were not properly shaped for catching cod in the bay, but, again, Squanto solved the problem for them and showed them how to make new ones.

In due time Massasoit made a visit to the colony, the treaty was signed, the pipe of peace was smoked, and the great chief left very pleased, for the Narragansetts, his enemies across the bay, would now be more fearful of attacking him.

As the *Mayflower* became more and more deserted, Priscilla was finally prevailed upon to leave her family's cubicle. The other girls had already left the captain's cabin and were living in curtained-off quarters in the Common House.

The Brewsters, who had completed building their house, did not feel it right for a young woman like Priscilla to be on the ship unguarded. Priscilla could not tell them that as long as Alden was there she felt somehow safe. Even though Priscilla kept an impersonal attitude toward him, she could tell he would like it to be different. She still deeply felt the loss of her family and could not forget the scene between Desire and John, and so she kept a space between them.

Desire had lately been more and more with the two Edwards, Dotey and Leister, but Priscilla did not miss the glow in her eyes whenever John was around. So, on the last evening aboard ship, she went up on deck after she had finished packing, partly as a final gesture to the memories there and partly in hopes of finding John. The ship rocked gently in the quiet twilight, the glow of its orange lantern small but warm against enormous indigo blue clouds piled high on a sapphire sky. It was peaceful and soothing, and Priscilla almost wished she could sail forever like this—a ghost on a ghost ship. She stayed there, hearing the murmur of voices in the cabins above until the chilling breeze closed off all the memories of the long voyage overseas, and she was alone.

Priscilla would sleep hardly at all the first night in the Brewsters' house, although they had certainly tried to make her feel welcome. A large corner of the main room was curtained off—more than she needed, she kept telling Mary Brewster.

"Now let us spoil thee a little," Mary answered. "Ye will comfort us for our older daughter who is married and did not come with us."—and she gave Priscilla a gentle hug.

The furniture, to be sure, was sparse, but after living on the *Mayflower* it appeared luxurious. The dirt floor had been swept clean with a cornstalk broom and tramped hard by the little boys. A large rug had been placed in the center of the lower area and one also in Priscilla's "room." The stone chimney was only halfway finished, but there were already ashes in the fireplace where it had been tried out. The cooking hooks were in, and also the pots were placed in order. All of these things and the trestle table and benches made the place look home-like. A wooden washtub stood in a corner. There were also a butter churn and a spinning wheel standing ready but both useless since as yet there was no cream to churn and no flax to spin.

The Brewsters had brought their large oak bed and dresser which stood in a corner of their little room. The two boys were sleeping in the loft.

Priscilla's eyes filled with tears when she saw that they had had her parents' own bed and wardrobe brought in from the ship for her. "We have arranged for all the rest of thy family goods to be stored in the Common House for a while," Elder Brewster kindly told her, putting his arms around her shoulders.

The little boys were behaving wildly with a guest in the house. They both wanted her attention at once, Love grabbing one hand and Wrassle pulling the other. They nearly pulled her off the ladder into the loft, as eager as they were to have her see their "captain's cabin."

Dinner was merry and hearty. The boys started calling her Priscilla but were admonished to show her a little more respect. "Ye may call her 'sister,' if ye wish, or 'Mistress Priscilla' . . . and boys . . . calm thyselves," their mother said when they jumped and twisted as they sat on the bench at dinner, shaking Priscilla so she spilled her cup of tea. It hurt her a little to see them for they reminded her so much of Joseph.

Afterwards, prayers were said as they sat in a circle, holding hands, just as Priscilla's own family had done. Then, under protest, the boys scrambled up the ladder, tossed their blankets and pillows at each other, and suddenly were quiet as darkness settled into the little house and candles were lit.

"Come outside with us, Priscilla, dear," Mary called as Priscilla was carrying the plates to the hutch. "The reflection of the sunset in the clouds over the sea is just beautiful tonight."

Priscilla joined her and listened to the sounds of the evening, the rhythm of the waves as they whispered when they reached the sand, the muffled sound of laughter from a nearby house, and the quiet chirping of sleepy birds. She watched as a transparent haze crept across the water almost like a live spirit and darkness stole up to the house.

Perhaps it was the contrast between the warm gaiety of the supper and the cold, enclosed blackness of the room, but, when Priscilla awakened suddenly in the night, terror grasped her. In her nightmare she had heard her mother calling her.

She had searched everywhere but had not been able to find her.

There was absolutely no sound whatever in the strange house. She was not accustomed to the stillness and the absence of the sound of waves lapping the hull of the ship on which she had spent the last seven months. She missed the security of knowing that John Alden was nearby, and the fear that he might return to England with the ship, after all, made her feel cold in the new bed. Then she heard one of the little boys turn over with a sigh, talking to himself, and somehow she managed to fall asleep again.

One morning in early April, John Howland came running up the path between the five little houses that had been built, shouting: "The tide's going out! The ship's leaving!"

Mary and Priscilla dropped the berries they were fixing, snatching shawls and cloaks and running down to the shore with Elder Brewster and the rest. The men in the field dropped their axes and hoes and ran after the group.

Standing with Captain Jones were Brewster, Bradford, Allerton, Winslow, and Alden. The *Mayflower* shore boat was beached close by with two sailors waiting to take the captain back to the ship.

Priscilla stood silently with the others, watching Alden. She had tried to find out from Elder Brewster and some others what his plans were, but he seemed not to have discussed the matter with anyone.

"Give this letter to Thomas Weston," Brewster was saying to the captain. "He is handling the contract whereby we are to receive supplies and further bartering material by the next ship coming across."

"The merchants will expect furs, lumber, and fish from ye, ye are well aware," the captain pointed out.

"Ye will have to tell them what has happened to us . . . how we have lost half our people through scurvy and this dread disease."

"I will tell them . . . I will do my best."

"Ye have been good to keep your ship in harbor so long for our sakes," Bradford added.

"In truth," the captain said with a wry smile, "I could not have taken her to home port sooner for I have lost many men and could not risk facing a gale."

"Then farewell, friend. A good voyage and Godspeed."

Brewster and the captain embraced.

"Farewell to ye, too," Jones said, addressing the entire group. "May ye stay in good health and your settlement prosper."

Priscilla held her breath as Alden went to the small boat with Jones. He waited while the captain got in—then shook his hand.

"We shall miss ye, Alden," Jones said. "Ye were a good hand to have aboard. I personally shall miss ye."

"Thank ye, sir," Alden said as he pushed the boat off.

"May ye, Alden, find happiness here,"—and the captain looked straight at Priscilla—"and may ye *all* find your haven of freedom in this place." He waved, and the onlookers on the shore waved back and watched him as he was rowed out and boarded the *Mayflower*. Soon the sails on the ship began to rise. There was silence and a strange feeling of loss and loneliness. Some of the women began to weep, but Priscilla felt only gladness and relief as John came back up the beach, looking at her.

Then, as the *Mayflower* started to sail away, Bradford stepped up onto a sandy ledge and addressed the settlers.

"We are all one group of colonists now . . . planters and pilgrims in a new land. We are alone in an alien encampment.

It is our joy that none of ye . . . not one . . . chose to return to England . . . and our further joy that so many of ye have returned to health . . . and that so many have joined the faith. But now the time has come, if we are to survive . . . for hard work! No man or woman or child over ten is to have idle hands . . . is that understood? Now let us return to work with zeal and dedication and God's blessing."

As the company looked toward the horizon, the *Mayflower* was gone, but the sun glittering on the water, the seagulls soaring freely, and the puffs of warm wind soothed the parting, and the group went back up the hill again with spirited, resolute steps.

Chapter Fifteen

The gorgeous garden in Eden could not have given Adam and Eve more delight than the coming of spring did the Pilgrims. As the warmer weather came, the blue of the sky was curtained with leaves of green lace. Flowers burst forth on trees and bushes, through patches of snow on the ground, and even through the sand on the beach. The sea and streams were filled with fish, the air and woods with birds, and the forest with wild fruits, nuts, and game. Although the wheat and peas refused to grow, the corn came forth in small fountains of green. It was as if Nature were trying to recompense the newcomers for her original unkind greeting.

In early May, Edward Winslow came to Elder Brewster and told him that he and Susanna White wished to be married.

"I am aware," Winslow said, "that this must seem a sudden betrothment to ye and the rest of the colony since I lost my wife Elizabeth, and the widow White her husband only a few months ago. But I, having loved Elizabeth greatly"—with this he began to break down but controlled himself and went on—"am a very lonely man. And Susanna has two small children with no father, and neither of us has a home . . . we both *need* each other, and we are in love. We, Susanna and I, are nearly of an age and I have always wanted children, and I do like these little ones and will care for them as a father"—he held out his hands as if in supplication—"and I will be a loving husband."

"And is your feeling for Susanna returned?"

"Yes. Yes. We really care for each other. Will ye marry us?"

The elder sat down on the bench by his table and thought for a moment. Then he rose again and put his hands on Edward Winslow's shoulders. "If ye are truly to be a good husband and father, then before God I see no reason why ye should not be married. And I do not believe our people will be critical in any way." He smiled and sat down, motioning Winslow to be seated, also. "Ye realize this is the first wedding in our midst?" he said happily. "It must be sanctioned according to law, also, and I must consult with others on these matters as it concerns many things of the future. I will give ye the rights of the church."

So Brewster called upon Bradford to examine his many books and decide for possible further events what was involved in these proceedings.

"I will have to consult with Winslow, Allerton, and Hopkins," Bradford replied. Later that night Bradford wrote in his journal the reflections of the group.

According to the laudable custom of the Low Countries, in which we lived, it was thought a marriage should be performed by the magistrate as being a civil thing, upon which many inheritances do depend, and most consonant to the Scriptures, and nowhere found in the Gospel to be laid upon the ministers as a part of their office. And this practice has continued amongst us and been followed by all the famous churches of Christ to this time.

Thus Bradford was told to perform the ceremony with Brewster consecrating it.

It was a great occasion, this first marriage in the new country. Susanna White was to be the first bride as she had been the first mother.

Brewster had been right about the Pilgrims' reaction. Everyone seemed glad for an excuse for happiness. The women, especially, were delighted. They draped the Common House with garlands of fresh flowers, laid their best carpets in front of the new altar. Every woman in the settlement, even the little girls, embroidered the bride's wedding dress with a flower and her own initials.

Dresses for the women and fancy shirts and breeches for the men not worn for many months were uncovered from trunks, cleaned, and ironed. The tables were laid with best linens and even the ground in front of the Common House swept clean, and the rocks decorated with flowers.

It was a happy occasion after the long sadness. Widows and widowers dared to look at each other, and those who were single forgot their work and thought only of love. Although the young ladies appeared at the wedding properly chaperoned, there were many glances passed between lowered eyes during the prayers, and, after the ceremony was over and felicitations to the new couple began, the young people slipped away toward the beach.

Desire Minter was flanked by the two Edwards, John Howland held Elizabeth Tilley's hand as they walked, Richard Warren and William Latham were vying for Elizabeth Hopkins's attention, and Mary Chilton was between Francis Eaton and John Goodman. As Priscilla left the Common House, she saw Miles Standish and John Alden making their way toward her, but she felt a hand on her elbow, and Peter Browne was hurrying her between the wedding guests and out into the sunshine.

Priscilla looked back to find that Alden and Standish had been drawn into some kind of consultation with Elder Brewster and the governor. More and more, Alden was being called upon for advice on building and organizing the village.

He was being asked to supervise the construction of homes and the stockade in the daytime and to work on plans or attend council meetings at night. There were many problems regarding the safety of the colony, dealings with the Indians (who had become almost too friendly since they had discovered the delights of the white people's cooking), the collection and storage of furs, fish, and wood to be returned to English investors as part of their payment, and the many individual problems of the settlers.

There was to be a bonfire gathering on the beach in the evening after the wedding, and Priscilla had looked forward to it, hoping that John might seek her out. It started out to be a perfect evening. As she walked to the shore, Priscilla watched the full moon rising over the sea. Small white waves slapped against the sand and sighed as they fell back. She felt the summer breeze powder her face with blossoms and soft seeds. The smoke from the fire reached her with the appetizing smell of clams being prepared. She sat with the Brewsters, but afterward, when the big circle was being formed, she was sure John would join her for she had noticed him watching her all through the wedding supper. And he did come to her side.

Her throat tightened as he took her hand in his callused one and squeezed it hard. With his strong arm holding hers as they circled around the fire, she felt feather-light in the soft sand and wished she could run barefoot along the water's edge with him. When the evening's singing was finished, they looked at each other unsmiling, Alden's hand still holding hers until her face felt hot and flushed. She finally looked around, embarrassed, to see if anyone had noticed, but the group was breaking up. Alden started to pull her away and motioned to a separate path, when suddenly Desire approached them.

"Mister Alden," she said with a sweet smile, "I would like

to have someone to walk with through the dark. Do ye mind if I join ye?"

Alden hesitated a moment, then shrugged, not smiling. "Priscilla and I will walk with ye."

Desire took Alden's arm, looking up at him and ignoring Priscilla. "I do think that fireplace ye are building for us at the Billingtons' is splendid . . . so sturdy and artistic . . . the way ye set the stones and all. Ye will be back in the morning to finish it?"

John answered her curtly, and the conversation went on between the two of them until they reached the Brewsters' house, where Priscilla bid them both a reluctant good night. As she turned and looked back, she saw Desire put both her hands on Alden's elbow. She was so obvious in pursuing him. Was John really yielding and was her own love hopeless? She entered the house and was surprised to find Governor Bradford waiting for the Brewsters to return. He seemed to have been watching through the open door. He took Priscilla's hand and motioned with his eyes toward the two people walking away.

"Priscilla," he said quietly, "I wish ye could look at me like that. Ye have always been so good to me, caring for me when I was sick and helping me feel capable of being governor. Ye must know how I feel about thee."

"My dear Governor," Priscilla tried to speak carefully, "ye are a very attractive man . . . and any girl is fortunate to hear ye speak so. I do so very much respect ye . . . and it has nothing to do with the difference in our ages. . . ."

"I understand, Priscilla," he interrupted. "I had only to see the two of ye, ye and Alden together tonight, to know how it is with thee. There is no explaining love is there?"

Priscilla looked down with a sigh. "No. There is no explaining love."

★ ★ ★ ★ ★

"It was bound to happen," John Billington said accusingly to Brewster several weeks later. "The kidnapping of my son was bound to happen. The way ye let them Indians run about here, in and out of our houses." He shouted and shook his finger under Brewster's nose. "Ye and your love! Well, I'm just surprised they didn't take my wife instead of my son!"

It had been about five o'clock in the late afternoon when Ellen Billington had run weeping down the lane with her husband after her yelling: "The boy's been took! The boy's been took!" Earlier the people in the village had heard her familiar two-level shrieks—"Joh-hn! Fran-cis!"—up and down the lane and her usual scolding and muttering as she searched for her two boys.

But this was different. The large alarm bell was rung for the first time, the parting gift from the captain, the *Mayflower*'s largest bell. Everyone came running, housewives from their kitchens, those fishing from the beach where they were cleaning their catch, and those working in the fields. Bradford addressed them.

"Little John Billington is lost," he said.

"Not lost . . . *stole!*" Billington exclaimed.

"What we want to find out is where he was last seen," Bradford went on.

"He was at the beach about a couple of hours ago, tryin' to eat a fish raw," Edward Dotey said helpfully.

"He and John Hooke and Giles, my son, ate some biscuits after that at our house," Elizabeth Hopkins added.

"Stop this talk," Billington said. "He was *stole,* I tell ye, by that Indian came to the Common House today."

"That Indian came to talk to me about helping us find that large bog filled with purple berries we heard about," Bradford answered.

"Maybe the boy heard the Indian and set off by himself," Allerton suggested.

Billington shouted: "Those savages have him . . . I know it!"

His wife began screaming and wailing again.

"I saw him not more than an hour ago out by the stream where I was felling a tree," Alden spoke up. "He was carrying a pole, and I thought he was going fishing."

"We had better organize a search party, Standish," Bradford said.

"All ye men but Elder Brewster, Hopkins, Warren, Latham, and Francis Cooke, follow me. We'll start out where Alden last saw the boy. Those named will stand guard in the village. Darkness should be coming on soon, so report back here to the village no later than seven o'clock. Now, come with me," Standish ordered, and they went off hurriedly with Billington protesting loudly: "It weren't no use. The boy's gone."

It seemed for once that Billington might have been right, for two days of searching revealed no sign of little John. Standish and a group of his best scouts, including Squanto and John Alden, had gone far into the woods in every direction, farther than they had ever been. They had discovered new waterways for fishing, new ponds filled with ducks and geese, new hunting grounds, but no sign of John. They had questioned every Indian they saw. They had all seemed friendly, but none had heard of the lost boy, and so the village had regretfully accepted the fact that the boy was either stolen or dead.

Billington wanted funeral services held, perhaps more to quiet his wife—so some of the villagers said—for the poor woman was inconsolable.

"Whatever faults the family may have . . . and none of us is free of them," Mary Brewster hastened to add, "the Billingtons do love their children."

But Ellen Billington would not hear of any services." She wept and waited, but she clung to the hope that her boy would still be found alive, even as the weeks passed by.

Mary Brewster, Elizabeth Hopkins, and Susanna White, the only other mothers left, gathered around Ellen, showing her their sympathy, cooking for her, caring for her husband and Francis. Even the father was touched, thanking them a little gruffly but sincerely.

It was Edward Leister who went to Governor Bradford a while later—so the rumor went—with a story that, while on a long fishing trip, he had met an Indian far up the shore who had indicated in sign language that in his tribe was a little boy with white skin like Leister's. When asked where the tribe was, the Indian had pointed to the south several times, indicating a great distance.

"There was something strange about the way Leister told us," Brewster said to Mary and Priscilla at supper, "as if he hadn't wanted to tell us at all. When I asked him why he hadn't mentioned it as soon as he got back, he mumbled something about not believing the story at first. We will send Standish out with a group tomorrow first thing, but their destination must be kept secret so as not to arouse false hopes in the Billingtons."

The shallop left the next morning with Squanto, Alden, Howland, William Latham, and Edward Leister, ostensibly for trading.

Priscilla found herself getting more and more restless with Alden gone. She feared for him in strange Indian country for she had learned that life in this new land was very precious and precarious. Contact with some of the Indian tribes involved great danger, as Edward Winslow and Stephen

Hopkins had discovered in July when sent to visit Massasoit. The chief himself, who had been given a suit of clothes and a red horseman's coat, had been friendly enough, and also his tribe, although not feeding his guests well or being as hospitable as they had expected. The Nausets seemed listless and poorly fed themselves since so many of them had been wasted in the late great mortality three years before the coming of the English, wherein thousands of them had died, as Winslow and Hopkins had reported to Brewster.

"The Nausets live in constant fear of attack from the Narragansetts, that very strong tribe that lives across the bay," Winslow had gone on to say. "With the treaty with us, however, and having good soil and observing how the English were storing their food and were industrious in breaking up new ground therewith, they hope for peace and a good summer crop."

But what if the Naragansetts now have poor little John? Priscilla thought. *What if the search party has to pass through their territory or that of some other hostile tribe?* The stories of capture and torture Priscilla had heard made her shudder.

If Squanto and Samoset had not been friendly toward the Pilgrims, they, too, might possibly have been slain. Squanto had given them a feeling of safety. He had been like a brother to them since he had arrived.

It was as if he had adopted us as his tribe, Priscilla was thinking one August day as she and Mary Brewster stood on a bench hanging thistle flowers Squanto had brought them. Not having a tribe of his own and this territory being his original home, he was in and out of their houses all day, bringing this one berries or that one roots to cook. He had taught them how to catch their fish, where and how to obtain their furs for trade, how and when to plant to get the best crops. He had taught them the ways of the woods and the rivers and the seas. He and Samoset and another Indian friend, Hobamok, had helped also and were always welcome in the colony. But it was Squanto who was loved as everyone's friend.

Elder Brewster walked in on Priscilla's reverie and, observing her and his wife hanging the flowers upside down from the rafters, had a puzzled look.

"Now what can ye be doing?" he said, standing with his hands on his hips.

His wife laughed. "Adorning the house, of course. It's the new fashion." Mary looked down at him smugly.

"There is no sense to women," the elder answered, shaking his head and leaning back on the chimney.

"Squanto said we can make fine tea from these thistles when they dry," Mary explained with a wise air.

"What kind . . . purple poison?" her husband answered, looking up at the greenery hopelessly.

At that moment Ellen Billington walked in. She stood just inside the door, saying nothing, her eyes glazed.

Mary stepped down off the bench, wiping her hands on her apron. "Come in, sister Ellen," she said kindly. "What can we do for ye?"

The woman just stood, looking at Elder Brewster. "Is it true . . . what I just heard," she said after a moment, as if in a daze, "that my boy has been seen?"

There was silence, then Brewster approached her. "What have ye been told?" he countered.

"I was not to say who told me," she began, "but she . . . someone . . . says my boy is with the Indians, and that Master Standish and our Indians is gone after him."

"Yes, it is true," Brewster replied. "We did not want to tell ye until we knew more and, we hope, found the boy."

"She says there was an Indian hereabouts who has seen my

little boy. She didn't say where . . . but she says she saw the Indian, too."

"Who is *she?*"

"I'm not to tell. I wasn't to come see ye . . . or nobody." She paused. "Then it's true!" The woman held her breath and started shaking.

"Yes, dear Missus Billington. But it's not much to go on. Edward Leister communicated with the Indian in a kind of sign language, and the whole thing is very vague."

But there was no holding Ellen Billington. She ran out the door. "I'll be callin' my man," she called as she ran down the path.

"What is she talking of?" Mary looked puzzled.

Suddenly Priscilla remembered seeing Desire and Edward Leister walking to one of the fishing boats a long way down the beach one time, and getting aboard. Had Edward purposely failed to mention that Desire had been with him or just overlooked it? And why had Desire waited until now to tell Ellen Billington, living in the same house with them as she was? Even if it was not customary for a young unmarried woman to go out in a boat alone with a young man, still there was nothing really wrong in it. Perhaps Edward did not want anyone to know. Now perhaps she couldn't resist the temptation to impart the news.

These were not the thoughts she should be thinking, and Priscilla resolved to put the whole thing out of her mind as she continued hanging the thistles. Then she saw that Mary had been watching her, but she did not question Priscilla, for which Priscilla was grateful.

There was an attitude of strained suspense throughout the colony as the settlers went about their work. For Ellen Billington's sake, they tried to avoid talking about Standish's excursion.

It was late the evening of the following fourth day when a call was heard from the returning shallop.

"Hull-oo!" Everyone recognized Standish's voice. Elder Brewster jumped up from the table and ran down toward the beach with John and Ellen Billington and Francis close behind him. Priscilla and Mary and the others followed. Francis arrived where the boat was landing first. Little John Billington jumped out of the boat in the water up to his waist, and Francis waded out to greet him, almost drowning the smaller boy in his embrace. Then his father caught him and whirled him around and around in a wet hug. Ellen reached him and, before the lad could catch his breath, enveloped him in her bosom so that he was nearly smothered. Meanwhile she moaned and sobbed and wailed in a loud voice, but no one minded because of their joy at seeing him alive.

"Ye do look strange, boy," Billington said, holding him at arm's length. His hair had grown long; he wore a beaded headband and was dressed in deerskin pants and moccasins.

"Ye look mighty thin. Be ye hurt any place?" his father asked. "If they laid a hand on ye, I'll kill 'em," he affirmed.

"No . . . no," the boy spoke proudly. "They made me a real Indian like the other braves . . . the boys, I mean. Gave me a real bow with arrows . . . and taught me to shoot birds and rabbits."

"Now everyone go back to the Common House," Brewster said, "and let us hear the story and celebrate this glad occasion."

Priscilla had checked quickly, as soon as the shallop was close enough, to see that Alden was safely back. He looked directly at her and smiled, and it was all she could do to keep from running to him and embracing him as if *he* were the lost one. As everyone walked back to the village, Priscilla waited for John, and he quickly joined her. For once Desire was nowhere to be seen.

174

"Where did ye find the boy?" Priscilla asked.

"Strange enough, he was with Massasoit, although we traveled twenty miles in the wrong direction. But asking among the Indians we met, we heard that one of the tribe who had found him in the woods had taken him later back to the Nausets. He had been wandering in the woods for five days."

"How far have ye been traveling, then?" Priscilla saw that Alden looked very thin and tired.

"It's about forty kilometers from the Nausets to this place, and we beached the boat only once for rest."

Tired or not, Alden, holding Priscilla's arm, purposely lagged behind the others. Just before they reached the Common House, he led her aside into a dark glade where a small stream rustled over some rocks. He took her in his arms, and she did not resist.

"I missed thee, Priscilla," he whispered, his lips brushing the top of her forehead, "every minute of the trip."

"Did ye, now?" she teased. "And all this time here I was picturing thee in terrible danger every second."

"Oh, I was, but only from the flies and bugs and the summer heat."

"Well, ye are safe now," Priscilla said, reaching up and putting her arms around his neck.

"I have had time to do some serious thinking on this travel." John put his hands on her wrists and looked at her searchingly. "I want thee to know I love thee . . . love thee with all my heart." He kissed her gently at first, then enfolded her against him and kissed her again as if their lips and mouths were never to be separated.

Priscilla had to catch her breath, when he finally released her. "John, I am so glad," she finally managed to say. "But I was never sure ye really cared for me."

"Or ye for me. There are so many other men wanting ye

175

. . . Standish, Peter Browne . . . and even the governor."

Priscilla looked astonished. "How did ye know about William Bradford?"

"A man in love has intuition. Ye women aren't the only ones." He smiled. "Ye need not worry. I will keep the secret. And do ye care for me, Priscilla?"

"Oh, John. Thee knows there has never been anyone else for me."

He took a deep breath. "Then I would like us to be married," he went on, "and right soon. I must be off again in a few days with Standish, for there is trouble with a sachem named Corbitant, in some way allied with Massasoit, but a man who has a sharp dislike for the English, so Squanto says. He and I are being sent to attempt a peace with him, but we do not hold out much hope in that quarter."

Priscilla turned her head away thoughtfully. "I wish ye were not one of the guard, John, for ye are always in such danger."

"But ye knew that the colony would need defending when ye came to this country," he said gently.

"Yes, but I somehow thought it would be others. There were so many things I didn't expect," she continued sorrowfully.

"I know . . . and I want to help thee forget some of thy sadness." He kissed her hair on the top of her head. "We will be married as soon as I get back and can build us a house."

"Mister Alden, my friend, and when will that be? Ye have promised half the people to build their houses already. Soft-hearted ye are, and probably will first build the stockade they're talking about. 'Tis possible ye be putting me off." She smiled at him, but he looked horrified.

"For my bride, I do no such thing." And he kissed her and held her tightly against him.

"Come, we must be getting back," Priscilla said in a husky voice, "or Elder Brewster will think the Indians have us." She reluctantly pulled away from him.

"I think Elder Brewster might just have a suspicion where we be," Alden replied drolly, and they both laughed.

A few days later Hobamok came running into the lane, sweating and excited. He said that he and Squanto had met Corbitant at an Indian town called Namassakett about fourteen kilometers west, and that he had begun to quarrel with them and tried to stab them, but Hobamok himself had escaped. He feared, however, that Corbitant had killed Squanto. He had threatened them both and for no reason but that they were friends to the English.

Bradford immediately called a council meeting and it was decided that they could not allow their friends and messengers thus to be wronged.

"Standish, ye will take fourteen well-armed men," Bradford said, "and search out Squanto. If, indeed, ye find our friend to have been slain, then ye will bring this Corbitant to us . . . alive, if possible. But do not endanger yourselves on his account and see that ye do not harm any who are not involved. This step we take reluctantly, knowing that our colony could easily be destroyed, if we do not protect those Indians who have been friendly to us."

Standish, Alden, and the others, led by Hobamok, set out on the Fourteenth day of August. Once again, Priscilla realized she must wait and worry, wait and worry, and that this was to be a way of life; and so it would be until the colonists had the opportunity to make friends with most of the Indian tribes and had a large enough group to repel those who were not friendly.

No further word was heard from Desire on the subject of

little John Billington, but Priscilla observed that Desire was often in the company of the Edwards, Dotey and Leister. They had not gone with the guard detail, and Priscilla was glad that Desire had found company other than John Alden.

It was ten days later when Squanto's rescue party was seen coming through the woods. Priscilla, Constance Hopkins, and the young girls were working in the field that day, for all took their turns with the colony's work, according to their strength and abilities. Priscilla saw at once that they were carrying three wounded. She and the other workers hurried to meet the tired soldiers as they straggled home. Alden was not one of the wounded, Priscilla saw with relief, for those being carried were Indians. Squanto, too, was safe, and Standish announced that Corbitant was nowhere to be found when they had arrived at the Indian village, but that his people, frightened and trembling, had led the scouts to a hut where Squanto and the three injured Indians had been tied. They waited, but Corbitant had evidently fled and would not face the English. So they had returned home.

"The injured are to be cared for with all kindness," Bradford said, and had them taken to the Common House. As everyone walked back happily to the compound together, Bradford further announced a supper on the beach honoring Squanto that evening after prayer meeting.

"Tired as I am, I must kiss thee, girl," Alden said, taking Priscilla aside and embracing her. "We will make plans tonight."

That night, the colonists were relaxing on the beach at sunset, after the meal was finished. Children played along the water's edge in their bare feet, while the women collected their utensils and dishes and leftover food, and the men lay back and talked about the day's events.

John had brought his flute along and sat on a small sand-bank playing melodies for Priscilla and a few others.

All at once Desire came running down the sand and straight to Governor Bradford. "They're *fighting* up there on the beach . . . with swords!" She pointed to a spot where the woods came close to the shore. "Around that bend there . . . Edward Dotey and Edward Leister! Please come stop them . . . somebody." She looked around and saw Alden. "John! Come help me!"

Everyone jumped up. John, startled, looked first at Priscilla, then at Desire. Bradford, Standish, and the other men, joined by Alden, ran toward the spot where Desire had pointed, followed by the entire company. As Priscilla approached, she saw Desire catch John's arm and pull him aside. She overheard Desire, who had her back to Priscilla, talking earnestly as she came up to them.

"But ye have got to stop them, John, before they kill each other. I do not want either one of them . . . only thee." She was speaking breathlessly and hastily. "It's *thee* I love, and I know ye love me. If ye would only tell them we are . . . uh . . . committed . . . they would stop . . . I know it."

Alden stepped back with a horrified glance at Priscilla. "But Desire, I. . . ."

"Ye know the governor will blame me," she interrupted, "and I will be humiliated before everyone. Please, please, John, tell them we are to be married."

"No. No. What are ye talking about? I will do no such thing. I will try to stop the duel, but I will do no more." He tore his arm away from Desire with a frantic gesture and ran on to where the two young men were being restrained by Bradford and Standish.

179

Dotey was screaming at Leister: "She is promised to me, I tell ye!"

Leister, seething with rage, struggled to get free and shouted back: "Ye are a liar! She is mine!"

"All right, we will see. . . ." Dotey pretended to relax, then suddenly broke away from Bradford and lunged at Leister, gashing his arm.

Bradford jumped between the two boys. "This is an outrage!" he exclaimed.

Standish drew his own sword and brandished it over Dotey's head. "Cease this skirmish instantly!" he commanded.

The young men tried to continue, but Bradford and the others dragged them apart. Alden stood to one side, watching.

When the two had been disarmed and quieted, Brewster spoke. "What is the cause of this disgusting display?" he asked coldly.

Dotey glared at Leister. "She is bespoken to me . . . I tell ye."

"He is lying," Leister insisted. "She told me herself that she is mine."

"And who is *she?*" Brewster demanded.

Leister pointed to Desire. "There. Desire Minter."

"Yes. Desire Minter." Dotey seemed puzzled as he also pointed.

Everyone stepped away from Desire, staring. She tossed her head and stepped forward. "They are both wrong. They are lying. We are only friends . . . friends!" She whirled and held out a hand to Alden. "It's John Alden I'm pledged to."

Dotey looked stunned. "It can't be."

Leister spoke quietly. "We have been taken in."

Alden slowly walked toward Desire, hands on hips, and,

standing with his face only a few inches above hers, spoke loudly. "The lady assumes too much. It grieves me that I must embarrass her . . . but it must be understood that I have never . . . at any time . . . given Mistress Minter cause for such a presumption."

"Presumption, he calls it! And him leading me on and taking me into the woods every chance he could get." Desire turned and stared at Priscilla triumphantly. "He should be *made* to marry me."

Dotey walked up to Desire. "I know Alden to be a decent man and ye to be a liar. Ye have tried to make fools of us all, and to gain your own ends . . . whatever they may be."

"Alden is too good for this hussy," Leister added.

Brewster joined them, speaking sharply to Desire. "Ye will keep to yourself, mistress, and cause no more trouble for us, do ye understand?"

"As for them," Standish broke in, "they should be put in the stocks."

"What ye have done is contrary to the very basis of our beliefs, ye must know that," Brewster said to Dotey and Leister. "We see other ways of settling our disputes than by anger. Now ye have caused much confusion, misunderstanding, and sorrow to us all with your unseemly behavior with this woman. And ye . . . Mistress Minter . . . are ye telling us ye have acted immodestly . . . or even immorally?"

Desire, surprised at this turn by Elder Brewster, backed off from him. She looked at Alden, at Priscilla, then back to Alden. At last she answered in a low voice. "No . . . I have not acted so . . . not with Mister Alden." Then with one final flair she added: "But he did lead me to believe he cared for me."

"Enough, Miss Minter. Ye have said enough." Brewster himself showed signs of becoming upset. "If ye speak or infer any more lies . . . ye shall be sent back to England on the first ship."

Bradford turned toward Dotey before Desire could answer. "And the two of ye are to be put in the stocks for tonight . . . to think upon your improper actions," then he added more softly, "and we trust ye will join us again after that time as friends to each other and the fine young men we know ye can be. Try to remember it is, indeed, folly to fight and that many times today's enemy needs must be tomorrow's friend."

With that the company broke up. Alden stepped forward toward Priscilla with a woeful look, but she turned her back on him and walked away. She was remembering the scene between Desire and John on the ship and wondering if there could be some truth in Desire's accusation. After all, hadn't there been much talk of marriage between herself and John and never a date set. Perhaps she was being distrustful and unfair, but she needed time to think.

Chapter Sixteen

The governor had impressed upon the colonists the importance of gathering and storing as much food as possible now that September had arrived, remembering the long, icy winter of the year before. The building of much-needed homes for the single men had to be postponed so that underground cellars could be constructed for perishables such as fresh fruits, fowl, fish, venison, rabbits, and bear meat. Storehouses were needed for corn, nuts, seeds, dried fruits, squash, pumpkins, and roots. They had discovered seeds to be of great importance, since the grains from England had not grown, for one reason or another, in the new Plymouth.

Seeds were not only necessary for planting but also for eating. The corn, especially, could be ground and made into many good dishes, and pumpkin seeds, so plentiful, could be dried and fried with a little fat and were nourishing and delicious. Squanto had shown them how to extract a sweetener from certain trees and with it the women had learned to make many new kinds of cakes and confections.

The women were urged to forego their regular housework as much as possible in order to prepare the food for the winter. When the men were not building, hunting, fishing, or harvesting, they, too, were expected to help with cleaning, drying, packing, and storing provisions.

As the days went by, Priscilla stayed aloof from John Alden. They did not meet often as John worked at constructing shelters from dawn until sundown. He even had permission to work during prayer meetings and on Sundays, and the sounds of his hammer and axe resounded almost as if he enjoyed the disturbance.

Neither Mary nor Elder Brewster mentioned Alden's name in Priscilla's presence, nor did the little boys, although Priscilla often observed them watching and even helping him. It made her uncomfortable. She really had not meant to break off all contact with him, and, although she would not show it, she was actually miserable.

Miles Standish had been training each segment of the colony in self-protection and had felt it especially necessary in the case of the "young ladies," as he said. Accordingly, Priscilla, Constance, Elizabeth Tilley, and Mary Chilton had had a session with him in the further use of firearms. The practice field was alongside the storage houses on which John had been working. Priscilla had felt very self-conscious, and, in mishandling the gun because of this, had injured her arm and begged to be excused from the other sessions.

As for Desire, she had not been seen at all, which, as Mrs. Billington had told everyone, "was a mighty good thing for now the wench takes the time to watch my boys a bit, as she properly should, considering she's abiding in our house." When Priscilla heard this, she could not help feeling sorry for Desire and, summoning her courage, went to see her one day when the Billingtons had left.

At first, Desire was hostile. "What do ye want?" she demanded after her original surprise at seeing Priscilla.

"I came to bring thee some of this special thread I found in my trunk, for some of thy fine needlework."

"Did ye wish me to make thee something?" Desire asked suspiciously.

"But, no," Priscilla protested, seeing Desire's attitude and wondering if the visit was to end in further disaster. "It is for thee. The color is special and who knows when we shall get more?"

184

"Well, the next ship that comes will find me on it. I have a large inheritance to collect, and I shall do it in London in person." She motioned for Priscilla to enter.

"Then I am happy for thee."

"This place is not for me now that I have lost my dear aunt and the governor, nor is it the place for a properly raised young lady."

Priscilla started to object but held back, seeing it would be of no use to speak about the satisfactions of building a new way of life and planning for the future. "I will truly be sorry if ye go. I want ye to know that."

Desire looked at her, and for a moment there was a companionship and a sympathy between them that sometimes women find in each other.

"I wish thee happiness with John Alden," Desire said, raising her chin a little, "and I am sorry. . . ." She did not go on, but turned away.

"I understand," Priscilla answered, putting a hand on Desire's arm. There was silence for a moment. "I wish thee well, too," she said. Desire did not turn around. "Let us be friends," Priscilla said, and then she slipped out the door.

One evening, after the boys were asleep, Elder Brewster looked up from his Bible at Priscilla. "My dear," he began, "may I speak to thee as an elder . . . or as a father, perhaps?"

Priscilla looked up from her sewing with uneasiness.

"I will come straight to the point," Brewster said. "Ye are not treating John Alden with kindness. Ye have hurt him." He waited, expecting her to speak.

Priscilla dropped her embroidery in her lap and looked at him through the candlelight. She could not find the right words in which to answer. She surely could not tell him of her very personal feelings about the matter.

When Brewster saw her discomfort, he sat back and spoke reflectively. "Ye know, Priscilla, my dear, that a handsome young fellow like Alden attracts the eyes of many young girls . . . just as ye attract many young men." She started to protest, but he held up his hand. "Now ye do not need to deny it. Even an old pastor notices such things. Indeed, it is his business . . . to see to the peace and contentment of his flock. I do not censor thee, neither do I condone thine attitude. In truth, I notice that thee thyself seem a bit unhappy. Could be ye wish to change the situation and do not know how?"

Priscilla put her head down. She didn't cry easily any more, but suddenly she felt tears come to the corners of her eyes. "What can I do?" she asked in a small voice.

"Thee must seek a way to let him know he is forgiven. Thee must find it in thy heart to let him know how ye feel."

There was silence. Then Priscilla asked: "Do *ye* really feel he is innocent?"

"Innocent? Innocent of what? I will tell thee this. He loves thee, and only thee."

"Did he tell thee so?"

"A man does not have to say these things. Not to his pastor. I simply know it."

Still there was something about his voice that made her feel there had been some kind of conversation on the subject between John and Elder Brewster. She would not argue with the pastor. "I will try to find a way to speak to him," she sighed.

"Sometimes the most difficult things ye have to do will, in the end, bring ye the most happiness."

In the next few days Priscilla did attempt to find a way to meet Alden, but now it seemed he was either not to be found or always with others. It almost appeared as if now he were avoiding her, and she began to wonder if he were meeting Desire, or if she herself had driven him away for good.

Early in November, heavy, cold rains arrived, and the Pilgrims were driven indoors. It was on a bleak afternoon that Priscilla and Mary Brewster, packing dried fish and turkey in one of the storage houses, heard a cry from the beach. Mary went to the door and looked out, followed by Priscilla.

"Look! A ship!" Mary said incredulously.

People were rushing by, and Mary and Priscilla grabbed their capes and joined them, ignoring the rain.

A small ship was anchored offshore with its dinghy coming toward the beach.

" 'Tis an English ship," Bradford shouted. He had brought his spyglass. "The *Fortune*."

The groups on shore began waving frantically and were answered by greetings from the boat's passengers.

Priscilla noticed John coming down the path, and she smiled at him, but he turned away, and she was not sure whether he had seen her or not.

"The Lord be blessed! It's my oldest son, Jonathan!" Brewster exclaimed as he waved wildly to a young man, standing up in the bow of the dinghy. Brewster turned as Mary and their boys rushed to his side.

"And Robert Cushman," Bradford said in amazement, "with his son Jonathan!"

Edward Winslow pushed his way forward. "Brother John!" he shouted as the dinghy beached itself. He ran toward his brother and embraced him.

Everyone crowded around as the captain and the newcomers were exuberantly greeted.

"Look what I have brought ye!" Cushman pronounced. He pushed two young men toward Brewster. "These two stalwart fellows and thirty-three others for your colony." He gestured back toward the ship.

"Indeed, we welcome your arrival," Bradford said. "Come with us inside and let us warm ye."

"We could use some cheer and warm shelter aright," Jonathan answered, his arms around his mother and father, while the boys almost tripped them all trying to get closer to their brother.

"It was a dismal look your place had from the ship," Cushman stated to Bradford. "We thought to find a bigger settlement."

That night there was a great celebration in the Common House for the voyagers' arrival. Also the thirty-five young men who had been landed would add greatly to the colony's maintenance, work, and defense. After the new arrivals had been fed, the young men were housed, some with various families, but most in the Common House. Cushman and his son, and Jonathan, were to stay with the Brewsters, and Priscilla offered to stretch a curtain across in the loft and sleep there so the guests could have her bed.

Before retiring, however, Brewster and Jonathan, Cushman, the captain of the *Fortune*, and Bradford met at the Brewsters' for tea and consultation. The captain seemed quite perturbed, and Priscilla and Mary heard them arguing as they went about pouring the tea and placing food on the table.

The captain could scarcely endure the courtesies of the meeting before he exploded. "These men we have brought ye are not . . . !"

"What the captain is trying to say," Cushman quickly interrupted him, "is that, while they are fine young men, they . . . and even I . . . I must admit . . . were somewhat surprised to find your colony no farther along. As a matter of fact, I am quite disappointed. I expected to see a larger village."

Brewster could see Bradford straighten up sharply, and he hastened to speak. "My dear Mister Cushman," he began, emphasizing each word slowly, "did ye not speak with Captain Jones upon his return? Did he not tell ye that we have lost half our colony, and that we were blown far off course and have suffered cruelly from disease?"

"Yes, and very sorry I am, too"—Cushman studied his lace cuffs—"but it has been nearly a year since ye landed. I do trust ye have been busy this past summer and have a weighty cargo for us to take back for payment to the London merchants."

Elder Brewster, Priscilla could see, restrained himself with great effort. Bradford jumped up quickly. "See here, what do ye mean? Do ye know what it is like to live in a leaky, molding ship for sixty-six days . . . with water pouring from every crack, yet none to drink or wash with . . . and very little to eat for months? Do ye know what it was like for the women? Do ye know what it did to my wife?" He was trembling with resentment. It was the first time he had ever mentioned Dorothy May. "As for houses," Bradford went on, "if it were not for John Alden, none of the rest of us might be here today, for he has worked every minute of every day constructing shelter for us . . . and that with very little help . . . for we have had only a few men well enough to work until May."

Priscilla, who had gone to the loft, lifted her head. Even the governor defended John—and he must know she would hear.

"We had forests to chop down," Bradford continued, "planting to do, fishing, hunting, gathering roots, nuts, and berries from the woods for food, Indians to scout, guard ourselves from, and make friends with. All this besides building shelters for ourselves and taking a little time for service to the Lord."

"Making friends with the Indians seems a foolish pastime," Cushman remarked scornfully.

"That is where ye are wrong," Brewster broke in. "Not only is it part of our faith but should be part of yours . . . and, if it were not for the Indians, we would not have known where or how to fish and hunt for food or for the furs ye are so anxious about getting . . . and, furthermore, ye would have no return at all on the contract, for without the friendship of the Indians we would have all been wiped out . . . would have starved without the guidance of one in particular named Squanto in this strange, dark forest."

Cushman gave him a quizzical look, and Priscilla could tell that trying to make this man from the modern, civilized city of London understand their trials of the past year was impossible.

"Ye have not heard from me yet," the captain persisted—and he, too, stood up. "These be a wild band ye are taking on, and ye might as well know it now. Some even be ex-convicts they are loading on ye . . . so I've heard."

"Ye cannot prove it!" Cushman shouted.

"Well, when they saw what kind of place they were coming to, they feared to come ashore . . . so they stole away my sails from the *Fortune* and guard them now with swords and will not give them up until I promise to take them farther south or back to England, if need be."

"They are just wary young fellows with plenty of promise for the future," Cushman parried. "They are not only careful, as they should be, but vigorous and ambitious."

"Crafty and wild they are, with drinking and gambling and fighting, as they have been on my ship. And nothing of their own to bring ashore, either."

"What do ye mean?" Brewster asked, both he and Bradford astounded.

190

"No, they brought *nothing*. Even gambled away most of their clothes before we left port. Nor clothes, nor guns, nor any provisions at all have they."

Cushman smiled, held up a hand, and rose himself. "The captain is overwrought with the long voyage," he said with a sigh. "Two or three are a little wild but good lads, and they and the others will, I am sure, make good colonists. Meanwhile, the ship must leave in a few days." He covered a yawn with the back of a lace cuff.

"We do have some goods for ye to take back," Bradford said. "We had very little to barter with, as ye know. We trust ye have brought a goodly cargo and provisions, according to our contract," he added pointedly.

"This was a hastily planned voyage and one to make sure of your welfare and undertaken for no other reason. There was very little time to prepare," Cushman explained.

"Well, how much did ye bring?"

Cushman shook his head. "A few crates . . . two of food and three of goods to barter."

Brewster looked aghast.

"I was simply to come along to see how ye are faring," Cushman continued. "Ye know I desire to come here to live amongst ye as soon as my affairs in London are concluded, and so, of course, I would do nothing but plan for your welfare. Our brother Thomas Weston is in charge of collecting all things needed for your prosperity and has promised to send a ship forthwith loaded with your needs, and I will see to it that he does. Meanwhile the captain must return to his ship tonight and . . . I'm afraid . . . I am unable to continue our conversation, being quite tired."

"Please don't think us ungrateful," Brewster said in a kindly tone, "for we are glad for reinforcements, if they, as ye say, are decent men. We are glad to see ye, too, our brother in this project. It is just that we are disappointed that more supplies were not forthcoming with the ship. Now, Bradford will see ye to your ship, Captain, and we will let Robert get some rest."

The captain had not exaggerated. The new group seemed not to understand the great need for work and found all kinds of excuses for not doing their share.

"Yet many times I have seen them down on the beach, playing ball," Brewster told Mary and Priscilla, "when they should have been helping."

Nevertheless, when the time came for the ship to return to England, the men decided to remain in Plymouth. The vessel was loaded with good clapboard, as much as it could stow, and two hogsheads of beaver and otter skins, as the first payment on the settlers' debt. The freight was estimated to be worth nearly five hundred pounds.

"I promise ye," Cushman assured them, "that I will never cease holding the merchants to these contracts and conditions, and that ye will have a speedy return of another ship loaded with your supplies and goods for your trade."

"I trust that what ye say will be true, brother Cushman," Brewster said.

True to her prediction, the morning the ship was to sail found Desire on the beach with Robert Cushman, her trunk, boxes, and valises being loaded into the shore boat. Priscilla saw that her face was flushed and happy as she talked with Cushman and the captain.

Brewster approached her. "We are very sorry to see thee leave us," he said.

"It is best for all," Desire answered with simple honesty. "I wish to return to the kind of life in which I was raised, and I would only be a burden to thee."

"As ye wish, then, Miss Desire, and may God go with thee." Brewster shook his head resignedly.

Desire turned away, and Cushman and Brewster helped her into the boat.

As the skiff pulled away, Desire waved at Priscilla with a smile. She did not once glance at John Alden, who stood to one side, his face expressionless.

"She is the only one of all of us to leave," Brewster said regretfully. "The ship brought us few provisions and took away more than it gave."

"And when that promised ship of Cushman's will arrive and what it may bring cannot be counted on," Bradford stated.

Brewster gave him a wry smile. "Ye do not trust our brother, William?" He paused and started up the sandy bank. "Neither do I," he mumbled.

Next day, Brewster and Bradford, with Standish, Allerton, Winslow, and Alden, took stock of their stored provisions to date.

"It will not be an easy winter with these added men," Bradford said.

"We will be forced to shorten our rations," Alden stated, as he added up the inventory.

"Provided we have no more illness, we will be able to hunt all winter and that will be of help," Winslow added hopefully.

Alden put down his pen. "Squanto has shown us how we can fish through the ice in the streams and lakes. We know so much better how to sustain ourselves than we did in the beginning."

"Alden," Bradford said thoughtfully, "we will put ye and Standish in charge of getting these new men to build two houses to shelter themselves. Ye are *not* to do the work, John.

Ye are only to oversee. And Standish, ye are to enforce the fact that, if they do not, they will have to make their shelter from the branches of the forest. They have ample time and strength to accomplish the construction, and the first heavy snow will provide the incentive, with your . . . encouragement . . . Standish."

It was Elder Brewster himself who finally provided the opportunity he had told Priscilla to seek. The lovely summer evenings of fireflies and suppers on the beach had vanished. The nights were becoming chilly, and the sun set early. Whereas most of the tasks and undertakings of the community had been conducted out of doors, even much of the worship, it was now more comfortable to be inside in front of a warm fire. Try as they might to keep the space in the Common House open, it seemed that, for one reason or another, it was always overly filled. Now there were the added men housed there in part of it, so Bradford and Elder Brewster were forced to hold their council meetings in homes.

A very special meeting had been called, and the members appeared at the Brewsters' home as appointed. In attendance were the elder himself, the governor, Allerton, Hopkins, Howland, Standish, Warren, Gilbert, Alden, and Edward Winslow.

Brewster began. "We have found the Lord to be with us in this new land. He has blessed us in our outgoings and in our incomings. We have found sustenance and happiness in this place. Behold, as the psalmist said, how good and pleasant it is for our brethren to dwell together in unity, as we have done, and as we will do. He surely has made us to lie down in green pastures, and has led us beside the still waters. He has truly restored our bodies and our souls and has led us in the paths of righteousness. Let us then give a commemoration of thanks unto the Lord and set aside a special time for thanksgiving. We will have one day of prayer and then another of celebration. Let us make these holy days glad days. Let us come before His presence with singing and enter into His gates with Thanksgiving."

The entire group then responded with a loud: "Amen. So let it be."

Mary and Priscilla, assuming the meeting was about to draw to a close, began preparing the tea and cakes, but Bradford rose to speak.

"Chief Massasoit has been our good friend, but we have not been able to show him our gratitude with true English hospitality. Let us invite him to attend the second day of our thanksgiving celebration."

This, then, was greeted with enthusiasm by the council.

"We shall set the day, then, and Captain Standish, will ye take some men and convey this invitation to the chief?"

"That I will, sir," Standish replied, ever happy to perform his duties as a soldier. A day was then decided upon.

As the meeting closed, the women brought refreshments to the table. Mary set the pumpkin bread before her husband, and Priscilla served the tea all around. Her hand trembled as she reached across John's shoulder and felt him lean against her.

Soon the meeting started to disband, and Priscilla dreaded the moment when John would leave. But when he was almost at the door, Brewster spoke.

"John, would ye wait a moment, if ye please. I have some things to discuss with ye."

Priscilla's breath came short as John turned back, and she realized Elder Brewster was doing this for her and that there were only three of them in the room now, Mary having gone across the lane to talk with Elizabeth Hopkins.

"John," Elder Brewster said, "we must make plans both

for the religious celebration and for Chief Massasoit's visit, should he be willing to attend. I would like to ask a very special favor of ye. We do not have an altar, and this is something very close to my heart. It would make the meaning of the Lord's Supper more real to all of us, symbolizing, as it does, the table around which the disciples sat. Perhaps we could design it together, John. Priscilla and Mary will make the altar cloth . . . is that not right, my dear?"

Priscilla looked up at Brewster and also saw Alden looking straight at her with a knowing smile. "I would be honored," she answered, trying to keep her voice steady.

"We will discuss the dimensions tomorrow," Brewster went on, rising, "and, by the way, we will need ten or twelve trestle tables and benches for our thanksgiving feast, of sturdy wood, that they may be used outdoors or in. Also a shelter or canopy on a raised piece of ground for Chief Massasoit. And Priscilla . . . we will also need a cover for that, and also a place for him to be seated with carpets, cushions, and other regalia. I will send Priscilla to ye, John, with my ideas, and the two of ye can work it out together."

"That would be fine, indeed," Alden answered pointedly, searching Priscilla's face. Priscilla looked at him and her heart felt like singing and dancing, and she gave her skirts a swing after the men had turned away and started toward the door.

"One more thing," she heard Brewster say, "I don't believe it necessary for ye to work at prayer time or on Sundays. There is so much for ye to do in any event that ye needs must train some of the new boys to help ye and not do it all thyself. I believe I will see what Mary is doing, Miss Priscilla," he announced, looking at her soberly enough, but just as he closed the door and walked out with John, he leaned back in again and winked.

Chapter Seventeen

"The chief has responded with enthusiasm," Standish reported to the leaders of the settlement, "and has said he will bring a hundred braves, squaws, and children with him."

There was a gasp from the Pilgrims.

"It is quite a few more than we expected," Bradford said dryly.

"I advised them to hunt and fish and collect deer, turkeys, squash, and pumpkins and other foods for the feast as they came through the forest," Standish said with emphasis. "And the chief understood my purpose," he stated without a smile.

"Standish, ye have handled it well," Bradford concluded, patting him on the shoulder.

A general announcement was made to the assemblage on the following Sabbath. The planned holidays were anticipated with great joy and a feeling that a time of community Thanksgiving to the Lord was right. The gathering also was pleased that Massasoit was to be welcomed.

Great preparations were then made for games and contests, for singing and even dancing. Priscilla and Constance Hopkins and Elizabeth Tilley were to be in charge of entertaining the children, both English and Indian. Between this and working with John on what he called "the setting" for Massasoit and his braves and sewing the altar cloth in the evenings with Mary, Priscilla was kept very happily busy.

Brewster was too involved with the religious aspect of the ceremonies and asked Priscilla to be his intermediary with Bradford and Alden on the second day's activities. It was when she and John were alone that Priscilla at first felt awkward, for he remained consistently business-like and never referred to the events that had separated them and never mentioned their former plans or in any way made love to her. The tension was almost worse than when they had not been speaking. She felt frustrated and upset, and all her striving to control her emotions seemed to no avail. She could not stop hoping for him to show some sign of tenderness toward her.

The day before the chief was to arrive found the settlement looking astonishingly neat and civilized. Many large fire pits had been made in the clearing and on the beach, for warmth in case of cold weather and for cooking of the feast. November had been a beautiful month so far, and prayers asked that there would be neither snow nor rain.

The Common House had been decorated with garlands of colorful fall leaves. Sheaves of corn and piles of pumpkins were all about. The new men, formerly living inside the meeting house, had been moved into their nearly finished houses, leaving the space clear for worship. A platform had been built for the new altar, and the embroidered cloth, the tall golden wine goblet, and silver bread container gave a feeling of warmth and home to the room.

Alden had succeeded in organizing the new men who said they were not skillful in, nor capable of, constructing houses or making benches. However, for the first time the worshippers could be seated for the services. Tables were ready to be moved outside when desired.

A dais had been erected for Massasoit, with a velvet-covered canopy to decorate it, ready for the second day's activities. The entire compound had been swept clean of leaves, and the sweet smell of their burning filled the air.

There was an expectant aura of joy as the first holiday dedicated to gratitude to the Lord dawned, crisp and clear. The

Pilgrims gathered in their brightest and best clothes in the Common House. Even the children were quiet during the long ceremony in which each blessing the Lord had given them was remembered—the pleasure of mutual affection and friendship, the bliss of peace, the escape from illness, the satisfaction of food, the safety of shelter, the pleasure of love, the liberty to govern themselves, and, above all, the freedom to express these thanks from their hearts in their own special way. Names of lost loved ones were remembered, and prayers for their salvation and the love of the Lord were offered. The gathering left the Common House that afternoon, talking together in whispers in the early twilight, with a sense of accomplishment and fulfillment.

On the second holiday Mary and Priscilla and the women of the settlement were up long before dawn, preparing for the feast. The squaws were to do the cooking for the Indians back in the forest, but still there were eighty colonists, Massasoit, and a contingent of twenty-five of his special warriors to be fed here by the colony. There were puddings, pies, cakes, and cornbread to be made. There were fruits, both fresh and cooked, to be readied and squash and roots to be prepared. Although the men had dressed the meat and fowl, there were turkeys, ducks, and geese to be stuffed and readied for roasting. Fires were flaming in the early morning chill and venison and bear meat turning on the spits. The women were anxious to finish their preparations before the Indians arrived so that the entire colony might give its attention to the opening ceremonies and the games and contests prior to the feast.

As the pale pastels of the dawn began to silhouette the men on the beach and those still fishing in their skiffs, excitement started to grow. Voices that whispered in the dark became louder now. Laughter was heard as the women and men hurried about their tasks.

"The water barrel is empty again," Mary called to Priscilla who was coating fish with cornmeal from a large barrel. "It's still a bit dark by the spring, so get one of the men to go with thee."

Priscilla looked about, but not seeing any of the men nearby, she picked up the bucket and started down the path, then came a few steps back and took along her new musket from among those that were always kept nearby. The sun was just appearing above the horizon and coloring the haze with a golden mist as she started into the forest. The birds were awakening with small, sleepy chirps, and there was a breathless stillness as she went deeper into the darkness of the trees. She drew her shawl around her.

A rustle in the fallen leaves to her right startled her, and a squirrel jerked upright and chattered crossly at her. As she came to the spring, she leaned her musket against a tree and bent over to fill the pail.

Above the sound of the rippling water, she thought she heard someone approaching. Could it be the Indians already? A deer, a bear, or some other animal? Quickly she reached for the musket and aimed it toward the bushes.

To her surprise Squanto and John Alden suddenly emerged. They stopped abruptly with alarmed looks. They were carrying loads of wood they had been cutting.

"Thee startled me," Priscilla said, lowering the gun, embarrassed.

Squanto went on through the woods, but Alden came up to Priscilla.

"What are ye doing out at this hour?" he demanded.

"Fetching water as ye are fetching wood," she said a little sharply to cover her nervousness. "There is a good deal of work for the women to do this glorious day of Thanksgiving, and so we are at it early."

"Yes, well, fortunately the men have already been able to supply the meat, build the fires, and . . . bring the wood," Alden remarked with mock irritability. "And the Indians supplied most of the corn and pumpkins and melons."

Suddenly they both looked at each other and laughed.

Alden set his load of wood down on the ground. "By the way, how is thy shoulder?"

"My shoulder?"

"Yes. Captain Standish informed me that ye had injured thyself practicing with thy musket a while back."

Priscilla looked puzzled for a moment. "Oh? Oh yes . . . it is better now . . . quite well." She started to turn away. "The new gun has a heavy recoil, but Captain Standish says I'll get used to it."

As she turned for the pail, Alden caught her elbow. "Here," he said, taking the musket, placing it in her hands, and lifting it to firing position. "Let me show thee how to prevent it from happening again."

"But Captain Standish taught me. I was just careless. He said. . . ."

"Captain Standish is a fine teacher, I am sure . . . and a fine man . . . brave, sturdy, fearless. We all respect and admire him."

Priscilla looked at him, puzzled. "He *is* a fine man, as ye say. A very fine man . . . though perhaps a little rough sometimes, which he needs must be . . . ," she added hurriedly.

"Here . . . hold the barrel like this . . . *firmly* . . . in this hand . . . like this." He reached his arm around her, showing her. "Oh, not really rough," he continued. "It's just his way. He's really a very gentle man."

"I know all this," Priscilla squirmed. "Anyway . . . he's short," she blurted out.

"Oh, surely, that doesn't mean anything. He can't help his

stature, ye know. Here now, hold the stock closer and tighter . . . like this." He held Priscilla closer and tighter.

"And he's not very religious . . . ," Priscilla protested feebly.

"Oh, religious enough. I'm sure he will make some woman a very fine husband. Here. Ye are not paying attention. Hold the musket *firmly* against thy shoulder. Pull it back . . . hard." He was pressing her tightly against him and suddenly spun her around, embracing her with one arm and dropping the musket with the other.

He had been so quick she was breathless, looking up at him. She tried to push away. "Oh, John! Ye know I'm not interested in Miles Standish. Why do ye push him on me? Why can't ye talk about thyself?"

"Myself? Whatever do ye mean?"

Priscilla began to be angry. This time she succeeded in pushing him away. "Well at least he decided to remain with us and protect us. But ye! Perhaps what Desire says is true. Ye do not know I saw ye with Desire one night on the ship."

"No. No. She was after me. I do not care for her nor ever did."

"But I saw ye kiss her and call her a mischievous wench."

Alden lowered his voice. "I am going to stay. I even have the lot for my house assigned to me. If all goes well, the young lady and I who are to live in it will be pledged soon."

Priscilla gasped. "Then ye shouldn't be here with me!" she exclaimed, hurt. "Who is she?"

He reached out toward her. "Well, she's a stubborn one, and unseeing it seems." He pulled her slowly toward him. "I love thee, Priscilla, stubbornness and all. Will ye marry me?"

She caught her breath. "John Alden," she said, between laughter and tears, "if my father were here, I'd make ye plead and *beg* for my hand, but since he's not . . . yes, I do love thee, too, rascal that ye are."

They embraced tenderly and longingly as he kissed her over and over, her forehead, her cheeks, her mouth, and her eyes. Finally he breathed a long sigh. "Then it's settled. And I did ask the elder for thy hand."

"Ye did? And what did he say that . . . that ruffian?"

"Why, he said . . . 'Of course ye may have her, John. She's a difficult wench, and I shall be glad to be rid of her. But if ye want her. . . .' "

"Oh, listen to ye, ye deceiver."

"Ye won't believe how feared I was of asking, Priscilla. Do ye know I loved thee from the very first moment ye came on the ship? I watched thee walk down the dock. It seemed I'd been in love with thee all of my life."

"And I with thee, even though ye are a deceiver and a rogue. I will become betrothed to thee, but then I will wait a while to see if there be any more 'mischievous wenches' around."

"If I must wait, then I will wait."

"I was only teasing thee, but we must wait, ye know. I couldn't marry so soon after losing all my family. But in a month or so, perhaps in the new year . . . ?"

"Whatever ye say, but we will announce our intentions tonight. I will ask the elder to do it."

"All right, then. But now, Mary will be coming after me, thinking some wild one has caught me . . . as, indeed, he has."

They returned to the compound, forgetting the bucket.

Squanto came running up to the compound to tell them that Massasoit and his tribe were not far off. Alden hurried away to get into his suit of armor, and Priscilla joined the women and children who were gathering on each side of the lane, in front of the houses.

In a short while the company began to form. Alden and Winslow were in front, carrying the flags of England and of the Christian Church. They were followed by Brewster and Bradford—Brewster in his purple cloak and Bradford in a red one. Behind them came Miles Standish and the soldiers of the guard in helmets and coats of mail, led by Allerton and Hopkins, one playing a drum and the other a trumpet. On the hill the cannon they had brought with them on the *Mayflower* and stationed on that strategic spot was ready to thunder.

Priscilla watched with wonder as the many Indians emerged from the woods and came into the clearing, the braves in the lead. The chief, who carried a long staff decorated with feathers, was wearing a great cloak of fur, and his braves wore shorter cloaks. They came in a long line, loaded with meat and other foods. Behind them straggled the squaws and children, shyly lagging farther back as they approached the settlement and finally stopping.

As the two factions approached each other, the cannon fired, causing a moment's confusion among the braves in the lead, but the chief came steadily forward. The Pilgrims met him. The drum and trumpet stopped, and the soldiers fired a volley of musket shots into the air. Then Brewster and Bradford led Massasoit to the dais, and they shook hands with him very formally.

"Great chief," Bradford pronounced, "we welcome ye and your people to our colony. May the greetings between us always be as warm as these campfires. Ye and your people have been most generous to us, and so, on this feast day, we would have ye and your tribe join with us in our celebration of thanks to the Lord God of all men and with gratitude in our hearts for all that *ye* have done for us."

Everyone was silent while Squanto translated for Massasoit. Then the chief answered and presently Squanto spoke. "Great chief says he and his people are glad to be here at this season of plenty. He has glad heart for your friendship and protection and for the treaty between ye. May our two tribes live long together in peace."

"Tell your chief," Bradford responded, "that now we wish to present some gifts to him and his people."

Allerton and Alden went into the Common House and brought forth boxes and baskets to Bradford. He opened one of them, and, taking out jewelry and long necklaces, he placed a circle of bright garnets over Massasoit's head. He then opened others, displaying pillows, lace cloths, robes, coats, and fabrics, giving each of the boxes and baskets in turn to the braves in attendance.

Massasoit accepted the gifts proudly and talked to Squanto.

"Chief says he gives many thanks through many moons. Now he wishes to present gifts to ye."

Massasoit clapped his hands and from the woods came braves bearing many furs that they placed before Bradford. The Pilgrims gasped when they saw their beauty.

"These are, indeed, welcome and generous presents. We thank ye." Bradford bowed graciously to the chief, then turned to the gathering. "Now let the games begin."

The men of the colony gave a loud cheer, startling the Indians, but as soon as Squanto had translated, the braves drew themselves up proudly.

"Let us go to the beach," Bradford said, leading the chief to a place among the rocks where cushions had made a comfortable vantage point for him.

All the mid-morning and afternoon the men took part in contests of archery, pitching the bar, and racing. Brewster and Bradford had wisely planned for some of the events to be by mixed contesting teams, with some English and some Indians on each. The race most enjoyed by the braves was the relay race, and they wished to do this again and again until the English dropped with fatigue and the Indian teams continued the contest among themselves. Accustomed as the Indians were to the long treks through the forests, they had fantastic endurance, and this sport, which they had not considered as a game before, was much to their liking.

Meanwhile Squanto had persuaded some of the Indian women and children to come to the clearing where Priscilla and the other young English women had gathered the English children to sing and perform some of their country dances. The Indian boys soon joined in with their own kind of dancing. Then children's games were played, and even the little Indian girls gradually joined in.

As the afternoon wore on, cloths were laid on the tables, and the bounty of the summer began to decorate them. The smell of the meats and cakes and pies, the pumpkins and squash, the turkeys and other fowl being cooked in the clearing, and the fish and clams, roasting in the coals on the beach, soon brought the games to an end, and everyone gathered in the clearing. Although the sun was setting and it was still light, candles began to glow on the tables and in the forest.

When Priscilla went back of the Common House to fetch more kindling, Alden caught her. "Mistress Mullins," he said, "see to it that thee do not avoid me any more, for, if I am to be thy husband, I shall demand a kiss for every hour."— and he took her in his arms, and they embraced.

"Someone will see us," she whispered.

"And I would not care if all the colonists and all the braves should see," he laughed, then helped her carry back the wood.

Brewster and Bradford were standing on the dais in front

of Massasoit, who was seated, and other Pilgrims stood below, coming together around the tables. Brewster spoke first.

"Before we commence, I wish to share with ye some tidings of much joy. It is my especial pleasure to announce the betrothal of Priscilla Mullins to John Alden. She is as my own daughter, and I know ye will join me in wishing them happiness always." He beckoned Priscilla and John to come forward. Hand in hand, both smiling, they received the elder's blessing, and the colony responded with loud amens. As they returned to their places, the group whole-heartedly shared with them the good news.

Then the elder went on to say grace. " 'Love the Lord thy God with all thine heart and thy neighbor as thyself.' We have tried to follow these commandments as far as it is in the power of humans to do so. Bless this generous bounty of food which Thou hast given us and bless all these who are gathered together here that we may live in friendship. Amen."

Then Governor Bradford stepped forward. There was a hush throughout the clearing.

"The Lord is never wanting to His own in their great need. Let His holy Name have all the praise. We are Englishmen who have come over the great ocean to America and were ready to perish in this wilderness, but we cried to the Lord, and He heard our voices. Let us, therefore, praise the Lord, for His mercies endure forever.

"We have kindled a light of freedom . . . a light for other men to follow. For as one candle may light a thousand, so the light here kindled hath shown to many . . . a light for other men to follow . . . a light to be cherished and guarded. And thus we found the Lord to be with us in all our ways, and to bless our outgoings and our incomings, for which let His holy Name be praised forever to all posterity."

Epilogue

William Bradford was elected governor thirty consecutive times, with the exception of three separate years. John Alden was his primary assistant this whole time and acting governor whenever Bradford was out of the colony or on trips to England. Alden, Brewster, Captain Standish, Edward Winslow, and John Howland were his constant aides. Unfortunately, Allerton gave them trouble later by proving to be too covetous of land and money.

Ill-equipped newcomers from England were constantly arriving, causing problems for Bradford and the Pilgrims. Hunger was a constant trial. There were also regular financial disputes involving Thomas Weston and Robert Cushman, but Bradford remained charitable to them throughout. In 1630 John Billington, Sr., was hanged for murder, a punishment that brought sorrow to the Pilgrims, for he was the first one to commit a serious crime.

Edward Winslow was elected governor in 1633–1634, 1636–1637, and 1644–1645. In 1643 he became one of the commissioners of the United Colonies of New England. He was sent to England several times in the interest of Plymouth Colony. From 1646 he remained for nine years in England and held minor offices under Oliver Cromwell. His portrait, the only likeness of any of the *Mayflower* Pilgrims, is in the gallery of the Plymouth Society at Plymouth.

Most of the Pilgrims who survived the original epidemic lived a relatively long time for the 17th Century. Bradford lived to be sixty-seven and Brewster to sixty-three. Priscilla died at eighty-two and Alden at eighty-four. They had twelve children. Doubtless Priscilla spent much time at her spinning wheel once the colony was able to grow flax.

Priscilla and John Alden were married in February of 1622. Desire Winter's name and age are included in Governor William Bradford's book, OF PLIMOUTH PLANTATION, on the passenger list. The Society of *Mayflower* Descendants' records shows that she returned to England, but the exact date is not known. She set out from Leyden with the original Separatists who had been in exile in Holland for twelve years. Records show she might have been Governor Carver's niece or grandniece. There was an actual duel fought on the beach with short swords between Leister and Dotey. William Bradford's son came from England in the summer of 1622. The governor married Alice Carpenter Southworth, the sweetheart of his youth, on August 14, 1623. Alice had two boys of her own, and she and William had one other child.

In spite of the firm foundation Bradford and Brewster gave the settlement, the Pilgrims continued to struggle with hunger in 1622 and for many years afterward. Their plight was augmented by another colony Thomas Weston had started to the north of them with many "able and lusty" men he'd brought on another boat. They went through their provisions rapidly and, because of their wrongful treatment of Massasoit's tribe, were in constant danger. Captain Standish was sent to rescue them with his guards and with supplies from the Pilgrims' own meager provisions.

The Weston colony failed in 1623, and the disillusioned men left the area after being given a small fishing boat and further food by the Pilgrims. They hoped to find other settlers to the south, perhaps in Virginia.

Mayflower Passenger List

Ages, where known, are given in parentheses after each name. An asterisk (*) denotes that the person died during the first winter. An (L) denotes that the person was among the passengers who set out from Leyden in the first place.

1. Alden, Mr. John (21)
2. Alderton, Mr. John (21)
3. Allerton, Master Bartholomew (8L)
4. Allerton, Mr. Isaac (34L)
5. Allerton, Miss Mary (4L)
6. Allerton, Mrs. Mary Norris (32L)
7. Allerton, Miss Remember (6L)
8. Billington, Mrs. Ellen (32L)
9. Billington, Master Francis (8)
10. Billington, Mr. John (36)
11. Billington, Master John (6)
12. Bradford, Mrs. Dorothy May (23L)
13. Bradford, Elder William (31L)
14. Brewster, Elder William (54L)
15. Brewster, Master Wrestling (6L)
16. Brewster, Master Love (9L)
17. Brewster, Mrs. Mary (52L)
18. Britteridge, Mr. Richard (21L)
19. Browne, Mr. Peter (20L)
20. Butten, Mr. William (22L died at sea)
21. Carter, Mr. Robert *
22. Carver, Deacon John (54L)

23.   Carver, Mrs. Catherine White Legatt (40L)★
24.   Chilton, Mr. James (57)★
25.   Chilton, Miss Mary (15)
26.   Chilton, Mrs. Susanna ★
27.   Clarke, Mr. Richard (L)★
28.   Cooke, Mr. Francis (43L)
29.   Cooke, Master John (8L)
30.   Cooper, Miss Humility (8)
31.   Crackston, Mr. John (35L)★
32.   Crackston, Master John
33.   Cotey, Mr. Edward (27)
34.   Eaton, Mr. Francis (35L)
35.   Eaton, Mrs. Sarah (30L)★
36.   Eaton, Master Samuel (infant)
37.   Ely, Mr. (Seaman)
38.   English, Mr. Thomas (30)★
39.   Fletcher, Mr. Moses (38L)★
40.   Fuller, Mrs. Ann (L)★
41.   Fuller, Mr. Edward (25?35?L)★
42.   Fuller, Master Samuel (5L)
43.   Fuller, Dr. Samuel (35L)
44.   Gardiner, Mr. Richard (20)
45.   Goodman, Mr. John (25L)
46.   Holbeck, Mr. William (L)★
47.   Hooke, Master John (13L)★
48.   Hopkins, Miss Constance (15)
49.   Hopkins, Miss Damaris (3)
50.   Mrs. Elizabeth (20)
51.   Hopkins, Master Giles (13)
52.   Hopkins, Master Oceanus (died on voyage)
53.   Hopkins, Mr. Stephen (35)
54.   Howland, Mr. John (28L)
55.   Langemore, Mr. John★

56. Latham, Mr. William
57. Leister, Mr. Edward
58. Margerson, Mr. Edward★
59. Martin, Mr. Christopher (45)★
60. Martin, Mrs. Marie Prower (45)★
61. Minter, Miss Desire (20L)
62. More, Miss Ellen (8)★
63. More, Master Richard (7)
64. More, Master (brother to Richard)
65. Mullins, Mrs. Alice ★
66. Mullins, Master Joseph (6)★
67. Mullins, Miss Priscilla (18)
68. Mullins, Mr. William (40)★
69. Priest, Mr. Digerie (40)★
70. Prower, Mr. Solomon ★
71. Rigdale, Mrs. Alice (L)★
72. Rigdale, Mr. John (L)★
73. Rogers, Master Joseph (12L)
74. Rogers, Mrs. Thomas (30L)★
75. Sampson, Master Henry (6)
76. Sowle, Mr. George (21L)
77. Standish, Captain Miles (36L)
78. Standish, Mrs. Rose (L)★
79. Story, Mr. Elias (42)★
80. Thomson, Mr. Edward (L)★
81. Tilley, Mrs. Ann (L)★
82. Tilley, Mrs. Bridget Ven der Velde (L)★
83. Tilley, Mr. Edward (46L)★
84. Tilley, Mr. John (49L)★
85. Tilley, Miss Elizabeth (14L)
86. Tinker, Mr. Thomas (39L)★
87. Tinker, Mrs. Thomas (49L)★
88. Tinker, Master (son) (L)★

89. Trevor, Mr. William (21)
90. Turner, Mrs. John (35)★
91. Turner, Master John (son) (L)★
92. Turner, Master (younger son) (L)★
93. Warren, Mr. Richard (40)
94. White, Master Peregrine (born on arrival)
95. White, Master Resolved (5)
96. White, Mrs. Susanna Fuller (26)
97. White, Mr. William (28)★
98. Wilder, Mr. Roger ★
99. Williams, Mr. Thomas ★
100. Winslow, Mr. Edward (23)
101. Winslow, Mrs. Elizabeth Barker (23)★
102. Winslow, Mr. Gilbert (20)

About the Author

Eleanor Stewart was born in Chicago, Illinois. She was graduated from Roycemore School and attended Northwestern University. She worked as a model until she won a Metro-Goldwyn-Mayer talent contest in the area. The prize was a trip to Hollywood and a screen test, following which she was placed under contract at M-G-M. She appeared in such films as SMALL TOWN GIRL (M-G-M, 1936) and WATERLOO BRIDGE (M-G-M, 1940). She also found a niche as the heroine in numerous Western films, appearing opposite William Boyd in three of his Hopalong Cassidy films released by Paramount Pictures, as well as Western films with Ken Maynard, Bob Steele, Tex Ritter, and Tom Keene. She even appeared as the heroine in the theatrical serial, THE FIGHTING DEVIL DOGS (Republic, 1938). In the 1940s she appeared in such films as LOUISIANA PURCHASE (Paramount, 1941) and SILVER QUEEN (United Artists, 1942). She married Leslie Petersen, an executive in M-G-M's publicity department and, with the birth of her daughter, retired from the screen to become a full-time mother as well as working as a volunteer at the West Los Angeles Veterans Hospital throughout the Second World War. It was while helping to start a children's theater guild that she began researching the history of the Pilgrims as an idea for a stage play. As a result of this passionate interest in the Pilgrims in the early years of frontier America, she later came to write THE FAIR VISION, her first novel. After she was widowed, Eleanor Stewart married Maurice Greiner, a friend for fifty years, and they now make their home in Poway, California.